AF191946

Michael Kopytko

BAR TENDER

novum ✦ pro

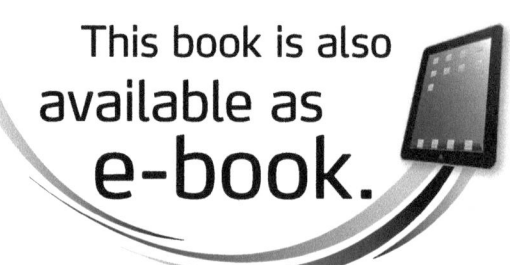

This book is also
available as
e-book.

www.novum-publishing.co.uk

© 2020 novum publishing

ISBN 978-3-99064-925-1
Editing: Hugo Chandler, BA
Cover photos: Michael Turner, Lopolo | Dreamstime.com
Cover design, layout & typesetting: novum publishing

www.novum-publishing.co.uk

Bar Tender

The clock had hit eleven p.m. by now and at that time, the moon rose beautifully over the Mediterranean. The breeze hit me in the face like a hammer, but I loved that salty sensation in the air that came from the sea. Dressed in a white vaporous shirt and a pair of pink shorts I was there to make an impression. I knew Alexandros would be there at that time, so I went with the perfect target in mind.

My sudden appearance was planned as a surprise; I wanted to see his expression once I landed at the bar. He knew that I was coming but since my original plans were set for the day after, arriving earlier was surely going to surprise him, or so I hoped.

In my head, I thought I would find him behind the bar or hustling around there, serving the clients; besides, this was one of the most exquisite gay bars in Mykonos, if not the best. The clients always expected to have an unforgettable experience once they arrived there.

The night was still young, and I felt that I had brought my A-game; I mean, I was going to see him again and there was no greater pleasure for me at that time. Our experiences from the previous year's still rocked inside my head; things I could not forget, nor did I want to.

Anyway, things did not go as planned. My surprise was slightly ruined since Alexandros was not where I expected him to be. As soon as I reached the bar, I noticed his alluring figure from afar. He was the same stallion in human flesh, expressing the same vigour and the same sex-appeal.

"Shit," I mumbled to myself, thinking quickly, wondering if I should hide or not. I did want to surprise him, but it looked like it was too late already. His keen eyes had spotted me and it was now pointless for me to hide.

I felt like a gazelle caught up in the claws of the lion with no chance to escape and really no desire to do so either. Like a magnet, he pulled me towards him and I could not resist this amazing sexual force. Gosh, I was busted, but I was still gonna surprise the heck out of him.

The facial expression! Yeah I still got that one despite not being inside the bar. As I got closer to the Mykonian City pub, our eyes met. Alexandros sat outside with two of his workmates, talking about God knows what. I am sure it was not about me, despite hoping so much, but that was not an issue anyway. His jaw dropped to the fucking floor like a fucking one-ton anvil dropped from a super huge crane. Alexandros needed quite a few moments to recover and gather his senses. Meantime, I continued to advance towards him at a steady pace, and I smiled as I loved what I saw.

His slightly hairy, classic Greek chest came out of his black shirt, with boldness, as if it invited me to do something naughty with it; not that I lacked such thoughts, but I imagined it would be slightly inappropriate to jump on him at first sight. I cannot say the same thing about him as Alexandros quit all prejudice and came straight at me. When there were only ten or twenty feet between us; he grabbed me in his arms with the strength of a bear. I could barely breathe.

Don't get me wrong now, I am a sturdy guy myself, I am not a snowflake, but I was completely surprised by his reaction and I did not have the time to react.

"My God, you said you were arriving tomorrow …" he kind of basted me as I tried to surprise him, but I felt no remorse.

"Guilty as charged!" I laughed, "Blame me for trying to surprise you."

Alexandros was not angry in any way; he was just a little bit 'surprised', if I may dare put it like that. As a result, I woke up with this suffocating kiss that came out of nowhere, literally; it left me no room to react and as a result, I just stood there like a sitting duck and took whatever came at me … and it was a lot, trust me. Those big meaty Greek lips almost sucked the life out of me as I enjoyed the passion and the love.

Pure desire and ecstasy slipped through my body that very instant and I could tell it was the same with Alexandros, as we both got kinda 'hard' instantly. Our last year's chemistry could still be felt in the air as our bodies boiled and rubbed against one another.

With the end of that kiss, a question emerged.

"Are you alone?" he asked me. His voice was slightly fearful and paranoid.

I looked up at Alexandros, whose puppy eyes had already scanned me for a reaction.

"Of course, I am alone; I came here for you. Remember what we talked about last summer?"

Alexandros gasped again. "Gosh, I thought you had someone with you this holiday, but it looks like I am the lucky one, again."

"You bastard, you worry too much. You'll get wrinkles and gray hair because of it."

My contagious laughter managed to touch him a little bit, caused him to smile back. He glanced at the fancy watch on his wrist.

"You have no idea how happy I am that you are here. I was afraid you were not coming anymore, seeing that August was gone and you still did not pop up … you let me know about your trip quite late."

He touched my hand gently as if he tried to tease me for a moment; I must say there was some success in his endeavour as I kinda started to feel those chills up and down my spine.

"You know I don't like crowded places that much; that's why I decided to go for September."

At this point, he leaned towards me, bit my left earlobe and kissed my neck twice … wet and gentle kisses that fired up my heart.

"Ugh? Really, right here where everyone can see us?"

He smiled. "I don't have anything to hide … do you?"

He knew he had cornered me right there. I could not say that I felt embarrassed in that position, as I did not want to upset Alexandros; besides, I liked being kissed like that.

"I guess I don't have anything to hide. I kinda forgot how non-conformist you were since last year and that I needed a little bit of time to re-adapt to that type of lifestyle."

I am not a puritan by nature and I don't get easily offended, regardless of the circumstances, but this was a foreign country nonetheless and I felt a little bit … timorous. Soon, the hug and the fiery kisses had cured any sort of spooky emotion out of me. I was back in business before I could even tell I was.

He grabbed my hand and pulled me towards him with a swift nudge.

"Shall we go in, I gotta get back to work; my break is kinda long gone …" He came even closer and whispered in my ear, "And … I have a surprise for you."

My senses fired up instantly when I heard the word 'surprise' that came out of Alexandros' mouth in such a sexy tone. Initially, I was the one who tried to surprise him, but it looked as if I was going to be the surprised one.

"Fine, I am coming, with no delay." I grinned and followed him inside the bar.

I stepped through the door, and found a packed atmosphere. Tourists and locals were having a great time, drinking, and dancing. All sorts of shapes and colours you could find inside, and Gay was king over all of them. Without exaggeration, this was one of the few places that made me feel completely comfortable. I don't exactly know what it was, maybe the perfect white traditional design or maybe it was the vibe that made you feel welcome and accepted. One thing was clear to me, Mykonian City pub was the place to be for people who wanted to experience the time of their lives.

With that in mind, I found myself a peaceful corner at the bar where I ordered a few drinks from … of course Alexandros. I was there for him and played no mind to the other people who walked by or danced around. I had come to Mykonos with a precise goal in mind and that was to contact Alexandros. Now that I had done it, I had little preoccupation with anything else. I was happy and I looked forward to spending as much time as possible with him.

A few shots later, and probably one or two martinis, I started to feel a little bit funky; my feet acted crazy and demanded me to jump onto that dance floor and show people some real groove. I thought to myself that I should have some fun at least while I waited for Alexandros to finish his shift somewhere after midnight.

Trust me when I tell you that I had no intention to hook up with anyone else, but some folks found me irresistible. At one point a tall guy; blond hair, slightly long, blue towards green eyes and a daring attitude approached me for a dance. I wasn't going to act rude, especially since he insisted quite a bit and I felt like dancing too. For a few minutes we danced to a few songs, some slower and some more energetic, but I did not feel as if there was anything else to it.

You know, we all dance with a stranger in the club every now and then … harmless gestures that are made only for the fun of the moment. I was not going to ask that blonde guy for his number or anything else, and I wasn't going to give him mine in case he asked. I did not even know where he was from … Netherlands, Germany, Russia … who cared really, we just danced for a moment and that was it; to me at least.

Other guys asked me for a dance that night, but I refused all of them after that first one. I had had enough, I can say, but what I did not know was that Alexandros had noticed my little harmless endeavour. He had seen me dancing with that guy, but he did not say anything to me, well not at first; because when I ordered another drink from him, I did not get anything in return.

After a while, one of his workmates came to my table and brought a mushy cocktail that was not even mixed properly. Alexandros was supposed to make it for me, and he always did them with utmost perfection. He knew his business better than anyone in the world. This meant that there was trouble in paradise, or at least that was how I perceived it.

My first thought was to go straight to him and ask him, what the hell was going on; maybe to throw that ruined cocktail straight in his face. The energy of the moment had taken me over, but then I allowed myself a few moments to process the whole scene again. I soon realized that to make a scene was the worst decision I could make. It could jeopardize my relationship with Alexandros for the stupidest of reasons.

As a result, I walked back to the bar to try and talk to him and to find out what was going on. I didn't expect a specific reaction from him, I just wanted to talk and feel his vibe at that moment.

With my cocktail in my right hand, I stood up and I walked through the crowd. I hoped I would find him quickly but Alexandros had vanished without a trace when I finally arrived at the bar.

'Is this the surprise he spoke about?' I wondered for a moment, but I knew that it wasn't. It was too nasty if that were to be the case.

Insistent by nature, I could not stand the fact that I could not get hold of him, so I asked one of his colleagues. That would take him appear out of the rabbit hole, as he could not hide his way out of it. I was right about that thought, and you couldn't imagine the wide smile on my face when Alexandros finally appeared. My mouth stretched from ear to ear, but I couldn't say the same thing about him.

Alexandros looked rather bored and irritated, but in fact, he was angry and bitter with jealousy … I would find that out a tad later.

"My cocktail is kinda weird don't you think?" I said those words with a bit of fun and sarcasm here and there.

Alexandros did not get any of it unfortunately. In return, he threw me this chewing grunt that confused me further.

"It was okay, but I guess they messed it up on the way to your table," he replied. I did not like his tone.

Secondly, I had no idea how a cocktail could be ruined on the way from the bar to the table ... unless, of course the waiter spat in it or something, but I am sure that was not the case.

"Really? Is that the best excuse you can come up with, for acting like a jerk?" I said with a slightly amused voice.

I wanted to tease Alexandros, I had no intention of pissing him off. We were the closest thing to what I would call lovers, and I did not want to mess things up between us. Well, I had another thing coming.

"A Jerk? Me? I am not rubbing against anyone back here."

Ouch, that burnt ... really bad and it reached right to my heart. For a moment, I had no reaction as I tried to figure out what I had done wrong, but the rubbing thing led me back to the dance floor where I shared a few moves with that same exotic stranger.

Nothing sinful if you ask me, but it looked like it had hurt someone's feelings without me even realizing it. Alexandros turned his back on me then and he pretended to wash some glasses, but I knew he mocked me. He wanted to avoid my eyes at all cost as he could not look me in the eye. His bad luck as I did not plan to let things rest that way... I had way bigger plans.

"Hey handsome!" I whispered, so only he could hear me. His black work shirt was stretched tightly on his wide shoulders; pretty sexy if you ask me, especially since I preferred to admire my prey from the back; a little bit of stalking, if I might say.

He ignored me. His ego was obviously too big to give in so easily, and the reality was, Alexandros loved the game and he would play hard to get to the fucking limit. He loved to tease me and he would torture me in the nastiest ways possible if he had the chance. I was in for it; don't get me wrong, I loved the game myself, but sometimes he drove me crazy ... in a good way, of course.

"Are you gonna pretend I am not here for the rest of the night, or is this is just one of your innocent little games?"

The words came out of my mouth with a special sensuality attached to them. I could feel him giggling slightly despite having his back to me. Fuck me, I knew I had reached all the soft spots on him, right there, right then. The colourful flashing lights inside the club blinded my eyes whenever they hit me straight up and the music had become slightly louder. I am not saying it was deafening, but that it gave Alexandros a good excuse to pretend he had not heard me. I knew this little sexy devil had heard every single word that came out of my mouth, but he pretended he hadn't.

"All right …" I mumbled to myself right before I dropped the bomb. I knew that I would make his fucking heart stop for a moment and that was exactly what I aimed to do.

"I shall get back to that dance floor then, those handsome steeds are already waiting for me."

I turned my back on him and I pretended to take one step away from the bar, and then I heard his heavy breathing at the back of my neck.

"Don't you dare make a move."

Alexandros threw the whiskey glass under the bar, almost smashing it to pieces and with that same hand that was free, he grabbed my right shoulder and pulled me back towards him. Shit, I felt as if I was pulled by a tornado. I did not have time to think about anything or even blink.

In a split second he had covered my mouth with his. I lost my breath instantly, yet the thing that 'suffered' the most was my heart, which started to race as if there was a madhouse inside my chest. That powerful suction rewired my brain in an instant and I craved for more. Alexandros tried to pull back at one point, but I was on a high roll, and I instantly jumped in for round two.

"You're mine!" I grinned and I fucking grabbed his head with both my hands and smashed my lips against his. I would suck up his soul if it was possible, damn.

I was so hooked up in our little romantic moment, that I did not even notice that some other guy was right behind me to buy something. Heck, I could care less about what others wanted as long as I had Alexandros right there in my hands, unable to escape.

A restless grunt that was close to a nudge came from behind me and that was when our second round ended. I turned my head slowly. My eyes were filled with surprise at this point and with a puppy eyed look I said, "What?"

This tall Scottish looking man looked at me with a disgusted gaze. I presumed that he was from Scotland as his hair was red and his face was almost covered in tiny freckles. There was a certain sexiness about his somewhat exotic look, but that presented no interest for me. I had not come to Mykonian City pub to catch something as my prey had been safely secured in my net from a year back. Of course, I am talking about Alexandros, my handsome Greek fantasy.

I moved away eventually, and let the red haired gentleman order whatever he wanted to drink. I couldn't have cared less about it, so I grabbed my phone and I checked the latest tweets while Alexandros did his thing. I did not want to look too obsessed or like a control freak; yeah quite ironic as I was in for a nasty surprise along the way …

As soon as the drinks were served, I turned to Alexandros who seemed to have had a whole attitude change; those kisses had changed the chemistry between us.

"So, at your place tonight or mine?" I winked, and that spurred a slight smile in him.

I guess he could already picture the action in his mind, and he definitely liked what was about to happen.

"I don't know…"

This mumble came out a few seconds later; it looked as if he could not decide on a final destination. As for me, I couldn't care less where we went as long as we went somewhere, together, of course.

"So, it's up to me." I added with a sexual grin on my face.

Things had already become steamy between us, and I could not help but count the fucking hours that had to pass until his shift was over. It if were up to me, I would've left the club that very moment, but you know, people must work too, to earn a living.

With nothing else to do, I had to suck it up and wait. I don't know why the hell it happens, but the more you wait hungrily for something, the worse the passing of time feels. This fucked up relativity of things killed me that night, and it did it as slowly as hell.

I felt like the prisoner of a forsaken goddess who drew her power and pleasure from tormenting poor souls who hoped for just a little bit of ecstasy. The worst part was that Alexandros would finish his shift at around six a.m. I had close to six hours left to wait. I had to endure the torture no matter what.

You can imagine that for the rest of the night I was nothing but a good 'boy'. I only ordered with him and I danced every now and then when a song I liked popped up ... I did all the dancing alone though, as I knew that I had a keen eye that always lurked behind my back. Whenever a handsome man approached me to ask me for a dance, I gently turned him down and returned to my Alexandros.

The place was packed with people who were looking for a good time. At some point, the air felt as if it was not breathable anymore, so I would go outside for a breath of fresh air. I quickly came back in though, as I didn't want Alexandros to get worried about me.

Just You and I
under the Shining Sky

Dusk was upon us at six a.m.; I waited for Alexandros to change his clothes so that we could get moving. Mykonian City pub had pretty much emptied at this point, with only a few overly zealous folks who still drank at the bar. I guess they were those sorts of people with an iron liver, you know; those people who could drink a fucking lake of whiskey and still pretend not to feel a fucking thing.

I looked at their slow tipsy movements, and violent laughter and I wondered what their secret was, but I did not get to ponder too much as my knight in shining armour popped up from behind the door that led to the back of the bar.

I quickly picked up something strange about Alexandros. He was more than twenty feet away from me. I could tell that something disturbed him. The look on his face had changed and he looked rather pale. His unbuttoned palm shirt that was drawn on a black background fitted his restlessness perfectly and made him look as if an angry tsunami headed straight towards him.

His walk seemed stressed too, as his feet smashed the pavement it was as if he tried to break it. I knew that I had to intervene and check on him. I walked towards Alexandros and met him halfway.

"Hey, are you, all right?" I asked. "You seem a bit off ..."

He shook his head without saying a word. Before he could take another step I grabbed his right arm. I could not stand to see him so upset, so I insisted ...

"Alexandros! Is everything okay? You look a bit weird ..."

I could feel that he avoided me at that point, but I was determined to get the truth out of him; part of me feared that I was the reason behind his sudden sorrow and I could not let that happen.

"I am only tired, that's all. People ordered drinks like crazy tonight and I just couldn't find a moment to rest."

His reply was far from convincing despite having a little dose of truth in it. His eyes were red and slightly swollen, a clear sign of fatigue, but his heart told me a different story, one he did not want to share with me for some reason.

"All right, I get it. I was there, and I saw how busy the club was. You need to rest without a doubt, and since you let me decide, we can go to my place, but first I have a surprise for you."

His eyebrows shot up at that point. When Alexandros heard the word surprise that had come out of my mouth, I could see his face lighten a little bit, and this was nothing but a good sign.

"Surprise? For me?"

"Who else, but you?" I smiled and I squeezed him to my chest. "You'd better hold on for this one as it's really gonna rock your world."

He started to laugh after this one, and that was exactly the purpose I had in mind.

"You've got some sort of magic trick up your sleeve and you are about to turn into Michael Jackson as I close my eyes?"

That remark almost made me laugh my guts out for a moment. Alexandros was a funny guy when he wanted to be; I guess that's why I loved being around him so much, he managed to get the best out of me.

I chuckled and nudged him towards the car. "You never ..." I replied, "my mouth is sealed at this point. Get in the car and you'll see."

This short moment managed to unwind Alexandros at least a little bit. The things that bugged him were still in the background, and I planned to get to them pretty soon too.

After I started the engine, I turned the car around from where it was parked. The small green Citroën I had rented was not the most powerful car in the world, but I could spin it with just one hand and it was perfect for the tiny streets of the island. It could get you practically everywhere you wanted to go … even onto the beach if you were a bit more insistent.

"So, where are we going now?"

Alexandros tried his luck to convince me to reveal my secret, but I had no intention to reveal it to him… at least not yet.

"We're going to our destination." I laughed in his face and annoyed Alexandros to the limit. "Stop being so impatient and let it happen … it's better that way."

My eyes shone, I could see them in the rear mirror; I guess it was the excitement that rushed through my bloodstream. I did not get to look in that mirror twice, as a different kind of excitement overcame me … a more sensual one this time.

Alexandros' left hand had reached for my cock and tapped it through my pants. I guess he wanted to feel if I could get as hard as the last year. He was in terrible luck this time, as I was rock hard … as I was so turned on that it would bite his fucking fingers off if it was out in the open.

"Daamnn …," he grinned as he looked at me; his hand was still there doing its thing, it teased me so badly that I could barely focus on the road.

"Are you trying to fucking kill us both?" I replied but he did not hear me. Alexandros was too focused on fucking with me, as I struggled to drive along the curves of the road.

"Uhmm," he hummed, and he smiled without looking at me.

"Alexandros, goddamn it!" I exclaimed in an almost horrified voice. "What are you trying to do?"

"I am trying to guess the surprise." He mumbled eventually, but I was on the brink of letting go the wheel and fucking jumping on him, right there in the car.

"We're almost there, for fuck's sake … please stop, you're fucking up my mind completely."

Indeed, we were a few feet away from the Folkos Beach, the place where I had planned to take Alexandros; for a swim maybe, or just some innocent making out on the beach under the beautiful shining sun of the morning. He knew the island like he knew his own palm and he could tell where we were headed by now … he loved that little secluded beach, I knew that for certain. The truth was, the previous years we made some quite steamy memories on that beach, on a hot Friday night.

Shit, it felt like it had happened yesterday; just me and him on the empty beach, the waves crashing on the shore with their characteristic chanting sound. The moon shone in the sky, full blown, with not a shred of cloud anywhere near and we were completely naked, fucking like mad men. That night was epic for both of us, and I don't think I could ever forget the feeling. No doubt, I would take it with me to my grave as one of the best; such nights make you feel alive and make you understand what life is all about.

As I pulled into the small parking lot close to the beach, we both saw the tiny tavern we used to go to. Alexandros grinned at me; his recent past drama was completely gone, and his face shone like a lightbulb.

"Should we go in for a minute?" he asked me.

I had no idea, so I shrugged, and I left it up to him. Alexandros looked at the tavern and then at me, then back at the tavern. I could tell that he was undecided, but then he made his mind up.

"Nah, fuck it … let's go straight to the beach, I don't even know if they're open at this hour."

At that point, a crazy race to the beach started; among the rocks and the weeds I chased him as Alexandros led the way to the water. As soon as our feet touched the sand, I could see Alexandros' shirt blown into the wind as he jumped right into the chilly water of the Mediterranean.

"You crazy motherfucker …" I laughed and I stopped at the edge of the sea to take my shoes off at least.

I wasn't going to let him have all the fun; ohh nooo! If shit was going to get down like that, I planned on being straight in the middle of the action. We were both great swimmers so there was no issue about that aspect.

After swimming a few feet away from the shore, and plunging under the water, Alexandros emerged back up and he turned his face towards me.

"Come on Mike, what are you waiting for? The water is perfect for a morning swim."

Slightly hesitant at the edge of the sea, I dug my feet into the still warm sand from the previous evening. My eyes were stuck like a magnet onto the endless spread of crystal clear water that reached towards the horizon. Only a few small dots pierced here and there and these were other islands from the thousands of islands in Greece.

For a moment, I lost myself among my own thoughts and daydreaming, but Alexandros took care to wake me up in perfect time.

"Heeyy, you frozen man, get your ass in the water before I get back at you."

His scream interrupted any thought process and he urged me to join him. A deep breath was the last thing I did and then I plunged into the water and started swimming towards him. To Alexandros' utter surprise, as soon as I got closer to him, he realized that I was butt naked. I had left my pants and shirt on the beach but, as I swam I ditched my underwear in the water too.

As soon as I got behind him I grabbed him tightly with one arm. He felt my hard cock as it rubbed against his wet tempting ass.

"Fuck …," he sighed. "Are you crazy?"

I smiled and I rubbed it even harder. "Crazy enough to fly for thousands of miles, then swim in the freezing water just to be with you … I think I am if that's the case."

Alexandros was rendered mute at that moment; there wasn't anything he could say about it, as I had underlined the situation perfectly. Caught offside as he was, Alexandros turned around; he had a wide smile on his face, from ear to ear, revealing his perfect white teeth that were surrounded by a thick medium size cut black beard.

That smile was sexy as fuck and it would turn me on every time I saw it.

"If that's the case … I should make all your effort worth it."

"You think?" I chuckled as sat nose to nose in the water.

The beach was completely deserted at that early hour in the morning, and this meant that we did not have any uninvited spectators that could lurk behind our backs. We were alone and free to do whatever crossed our wild and horny minds.

Before I could say another word, I felt Alexandros as he started to rub my cock with his hand, right there under the water. I never had someone jerking me off in the sea … yeah, I must say we didn't try that one the previous year, and I gotta admit that it felt … interesting.

We fooled around for a while in the water, but it soon took its toll on me. The view was splendid indeed, but the water was a bit too cold for my taste and I started to feel the cold as it crept into my bones. I couldn't take it anymore, much as I enjoyed being there with him. I guess Alexandros was more used to it than I was, hence his disappointed reaction when I said I had to get out.

"This is too cold for me … I think I'll get out of the water."

"Already?" he mumbled his thick dark eyebrows curved towards his nose.

I could read the disappointment in his eyes, but that was it for me.

"I was just getting started …" he added but there was nothing I could do about it.

"I am really sorry, but I can't resist anymore …"

He did not like my reply, especially what I was about to say next.

"You don't look like you had a hard overnight shift anymore."

As soon as I uttered those words, his expression changed again.

"You have no idea how fucked up last night was …"

"Maybe I don't, but you can tell me more on the beach, or on our way home."

I said that, as I tried to convince Alexandros to come out of the water with me, but he looked like he had no intentions in doing so. A sudden wind started out of nowhere and began moving the few bushes on the hill … that got right under my skin as I emerged from the sea. I shivered like never before as I struggled to put my clothes back on, but Alexandros didn't even look at me.

Frankly, I had no idea that my remark about his work had hurt him so much; I mean, we all struggle at work, but it seemed that in his case it was pure hell or something as his eyes showed a fiery gaze.

"Are you coming or not?" I yelled at him from the shore.

Alexandros swam back and forth now through the waves, as if he trained for the Olympics or something. I figured he wanted to blow off some steam before getting out of the sea, but I was into a whole different thing.

"Fuck off …" He shouted at me and he continued to swim for a while.

Trust me, that 'wishful thinking' did not anger me in any way; in fact it actually made me smile for a few moments because to me, Alexandros' 'angry moments' were kinda cute and I liked to appease his aching heart. It brought me a sort of weird satisfaction, you know, like make up sex that always feels better than regular sex. It has a sort of twisted satisfaction and tension and makes you feel really good!

"I'll leave your ass right here on the beach, if you don't come out in the next five minutes."

That came out with laughter from my part; it felt again like that teasing game he played on me. I loved to challenge Alexandros as much as he challenged me, but at that moment the freezing sensation was the one that pushed me. After a long night at the club I needed some rest if I wanted to start again the next morning.

Alexandros came out of the water eventually; his perfect packed abs and his well-defined pecs made him look like fucking Poseidon himself. Small droplets of salty water trickled down his chest and his nipples were as hard as stone. All he needed now was a trident and the scenery would be perfect … well, maybe a few dolphins around his sexy ass and then the scenery would be straight out of heaven. It as if I watched a movie scene that rolled in slow motion in front of my eyes ... I just could not get enough of it.

Our short moment of bickering had vanished from my head completely as I looked at him; now all I could think of was to have him naked under the sheets in my hotel room. I think I even lost focus for a moment as I delved with my mind into the picture of his perfect beauty. The moment he pulled his wet dark hair towards the back of his head ... it was a fucking blast for me.

I gasped, as I thought of what I would do to him when no one else looked at us, and I even ground my teeth at that thought. Alexandros noticed my amazement instantly.

"Now what?" he muttered.

"Why did you have to be so damn sexy and tempting, huh?" I added and he started to laugh.

"I guess the gods decided."

"Ohh, those damned gods; they always play with my heart."

At that moment I got up from the sand and I tried to clean the sand off my pants; Alexandros decided to 'help' and he slapped my ass, quite hard.

"Ohh boy, just wait and see how I am gonna play with this."

He even grabbed my ass with the other hand, probably trying to feel how hard it had gotten from soaking in all the cold water.

"Hmm ... nice and firm as I always knew it."

"Ohh no, no, you are not doing this ... not here!" I chuckled and I raced away from the beach towards the parking lot, where the car waited for us.

Back at the hotel, I felt a little funky. I was in for some action right after I walked through that door; what had happened in the sea earlier that morning had fired me up, and I yearned for more. Playful as that whole thing was, I grabbed Alexandros by his collar and pushed him onto the mushy bed. He chuckled for a moment, but that soon turned into a grunt.

Just like a lion that takes its pray, I threw myself at him and I started to kiss him; my hands wandered and checked all the parts of his body, his cock especially, since I had already started to take his shirt off. For a moment, I thought that he would give in to my temptations and would stand there like a defenceless prey, ready for me to wreak havoc on his juicy body.

"Damn, I want you so bad," I whispered into his ear.

He moaned when he felt my warm breath next to his skin. His hands grabbed my waist and I really thought that I was already in trouble.

The expectation of what was to happen next gave me goose bumps. Shit, it could not be better for me, but then, it all went up in smoke.

After some more spooning and kissing, Alexandros gently pushed me to the side.

"Mike, I am sorry, but I'm really not in the mood right now."

His slightly sorrowful voice caught me by surprise; his face expression suddenly changed; now I was caught in between, and I really did not know how to react.

"Are you okay?"

Alexandros sighed and he didn't even look into my eyes. I could feel that he was distressed and for that reason I did not insist in my sexual endeavours. I figured that it was best for me to be there for him and to help him the best way I could.

"I don't know Mike. I have not been myself lately. The moment you showed up helped to lift my spirits a bit, and truth be told, I kinda waited for your return as badly as we wait for rain around these places."

Missing me could not be a bad thing; his words made me smile for a second. I knew at that moment that I had to hug him so that I could send him at least a little bit of my energy.

"I am happy to hear that." I mumbled. I then kissed him slowly.

At that moment, our eyes met for the first time in a while; we both smiled and hugged. It looked as if there was not going to be any sex that morning, but I didn't have any problem with that. I enjoyed spending simple quality time with Alexandros where we would just talk and share our past experiences. The thing was, we kinda had a lot to catch up on, from the year that passed since we had last met.

Eventually, we decided to order in some seafood, his favorite …
squid and all the other shit. I am not such a fan of that, but for
his sake I ate a bit.

Fatigue started to take over us both, and at around ten a.m.
we fell prey to the goddess of sleep. I could not keep my fucking
eyes open anymore. After a night full of drinking and partying
at Mykonian City pub, and a full shift on Alexandros' part, we
both fell asleep. Yes, we slept together like two lovers, but with
no sex happening … just rest and hopes for a better day.

I remember that I dreamt something that day; I could not
tell exactly what it was, but I could feel that it was linked to
Alexandros for sure. There were some mixed feelings involved,
without a doubt, and they spurred me away from the fact that I
felt that Alexandros had not told me the whole story. He seemed
different from the past summer, and that meant that I would have
to practice some detective work on him.

As I opened my eyes, a few hours later that day, I had to admit I could not see a damn thing; my sight was fogged and I even
had trouble as I tried to blink. With a natural move I stretched
my right hand over to the side as I tried to feel Alexandros' warm
skin. I tried once; then a second time … and fuck, I could only
feel the cold sheets. For a second, I thought it was nothing but
another nightmare; my eyes were open though, and it was no
dream! Alexandros was missing from the bed.

That sharp realization removed any fogginess from my sight
and I jumped up from my bed so fast, as if I was in the army or
something.

"Alexandros?"

My whiny voice pierced through the silence of the room;
a grim realization that I was butt naked came soon after. As I
looked down, I could see my cock as it dangled from side to side;
I could not remember how things got to that point, but I could
not afford the luxury of time to ponder too much on that sub-
ject. I had to find Alexandros before it was too late.

I called his name a second time. "Alexandros, where the hell
are you?"

No reply came back, and I started to freak out; I busted into the bathroom like the fucking swat team, and there he was, brushing his teeth with his earbuds on. He couldn't hear a goddamn thing no matter how much I yelled and he kept moving his head while he hummed his way through the tooth brushing.

"You little devil …," I smirked. "You almost tricked me into a heart attack."

His back faced me, and I could fully admire his tight ass; the white boxers that squeezed his butt cheeks to perfection. The urge to grab that firm piece of ass was almost unbearable and the grin on my face was close to having that urge met. Fuck me, I had to go for it!

Both hands ready, I snuck behind his ass and I grabbed his ass. Alexandros almost bit his toothbrush, but it was a risk that I had to take.

"Mike!" he mumbled, with his mouth full. "What the hell?"

I couldn't help but laugh. "I don't know too much about hell, but this is heaven right here!"

I squeezed his ass as I said those things, and I could not tell if he enjoyed my 'surprise' or if he was pissed off.

"Stop fooling around, I need to get ready for work."

"Work?" I mumbled with a slightly surprised voice. "What time is it?"

"Time for me to go to work!" He stressed it again.

I looked for a watch, a phone or whatever that would tell me what time it was. I could not believe time had flown so fast, but there was no drama about it really, as I was going back to the club with Alexandros anyway.

"Fuck me! It's already seven!" I exclaimed.

"Told you … I gotta go." He nodded his head and then he spat the toothpaste out of his mouth.

"Hmm … fresh." I mumbled and I went straight for the kill … ohh kiss I meant to say.

The fresh mint flavour overcame me, and I could not get enough. I kept kissing and kissing until I was left without air.

"Delicious!" I muttered and I wiped the corners of my mouth. "I should get ready too."

Alexandros nodded his head, as if he tried to tell me, "If you want to …" as if this would be a matter for a question or something … of course I wanted to; that was the main goal I had in mind, to spend as much time with him as possible.

Two Shining Stars up High

After getting ready, we headed for the Mykonian City pub. While Alexandros had to work, I waited for another night full of drinking and dancing; not that I aimed to be in the spotlight or anything, but my style would always come upfront and I got noticed by other guys without even trying too much.

I started the night light, with a cocktail at the bar … my usual corner, of course where I would order only with Alexandros, you know, for him not to get jealous and stuff. My plan was to have a 'tranquil' night, nothing out of the ordinary, just wait for him to finish his shift so that we could leave together … but … you know how the devil always sticks its tail in when you least expect it.

Suddenly, these two tall, blonde guys approached the bar; they were dressed classic with dark blue jeans and white shirts. Their heads were held so high you'd say that they had to bend just to get through the fucking door. I am no short guy, at my six feet and something, but these two looked out of this fucking world.

The devil I spoke about, pushed them to sit next to me. A quick harmless smile was exchanged … you know, the usual courtesy of civilized people. I smiled neutrally, as I did not want to incite them in any way, but it looked like that had already happened. Sex appeal is something you can't stop or control, and before you know it, you wake up to find a guy chasing you. Lord have mercy on my soul, that was all I could say at that point.

One of them raised his glass in the air, and he said, "Cheers." Your first time on the island?" he asked and I met him with a smile and a head shake.

"Nah, been here before … lovely place, makes me come back every year."

They smiled and looked at each other. "Maybe we'll return here too … it's looking promising already. Sooo different from the Netherlands … the vibe is absolutely magic and the weather …"

Now I felt like, 'ughh'. He spoke about me when he said promising? I am not too much of a threesome guy, but I learned one thing in life; never say never as you have no idea of what is gonna happen next. You might be surprised to find yourself doing some things that you once thought of as 'inconceivable'.

"Bruno …" The blue-eyed Dutchman stretched his hand towards me, then the other one followed. "Daan." This one had a mix of green and brown in his eyes, equally as beautiful as the blue ones.

From the few words that we managed to exchange up to that point, I could tell that their English was close to pristine.

"Mike here …" I smiled and I raised my glass in the air as a response.

"Where are you from, Mike?" Bruno asked with a wicked smile on his face.

I tried to decipher the intentions behind it for a moment but I soon gave up as it was impenetrable.

"Well, my birthplace is Poland, but nowadays I am travelling through Europe, here and there, letting myself be carried by the waves of destiny."

This reply and the casual relaxed tone of my voice pleased these two guys, who were not smirking at each other while sipping some whiskey.

"So, are you here with anyone?"

Bruno's request fell like a bomb in the ocean for me. I was just tasting my cocktail again at that moment, and I nearly choked on it. I had to take a moment to recover from the shock, catch a few breaths.

"Not really ..." I mumbled and I could see his smile shoot up. "It's a bit different for me now, I kinda found what I was looking for, right here on the island."

A jaw drop followed, for both as they responded ... "Ohh ... yeah, that's one way of having things."

Something told me that they were already hooked with me. I don't know why, but they were both caught up in the spell. At that point I could only guess, and I did not know exactly what went on between them. Were they just a couple of friends spending time together, having a good time? It was nothing but guesswork for me, and I was not going to ask them either; I did not want to appear too interested to them.

In this 'chasing' game, I preferred to be the prey and not the chaser ... in most cases, of course, as in life there are always exceptions.

We laughed and spoke, sharing things about each other for a while ... until our glasses ran empty and it was time for another round. I figured I should make a nice gesture and buy some drinks for the three of us. I enjoyed their company, and since Alexandros was busy almost all the time, it was good to have someone to talk to ... especially since these Dutch guys were fairly smart, and I had enough subjects to talk about.

My mind stopped for a moment, and I forgot while ordering drinks that Alexandros might come across them. Surely his reaction would not be the nicest one, yet it slipped by me.

"Three shots of tequila for the men at the bar!" I raised my hand up in the air and I ordered the drinks, only to realize moments later, when Alexandros indeed came with the drinks, what an error I had committed. My man's face was grumpier than usual, and I could sense the turmoil in the air already as he approached ... the vibe was certainly on fire.

"Your drinks are served, sir!" he said with a sarcastic voice. I mean, that level of sarcasm could fucking drown me if it caught me unprepared.

For a moment I tried to ignore Alexandros' cynical attitude, but he was on to something else, apparently. As I turned my head to the side, kinda trying to tell him that he could go now, but without using any words as I did not want to make it too obvious … well, Alexandros grabbed the collar of my shirt with his left hand. I was awestruck.

"Excuse me? What is this?" I ground my teeth at him, but he seemed even angrier than I was.

"What are you doing with them?" he whispered into my ear. He then smiled kindly at the gentlemen who nodded their heads and smiled back as if they knew something about our sexual endeavour.

"I don't know what the fuck you are talking about, thus I suggest you stop being so bossy with me, cause I am not your fucking wife, Alexandros. Take your hands off me. I can talk to whomever I want. Leave before you annoy me too much."

Alexandros' eyes boiled with fury, I could feel it and I bet he would've snatched me out of there in an instant if he had the power. I knew that he was the jealous kind, but this looked like so much more; I had not seen him like that before; the previous year.

"You don't understand, these are not people for your linking … you shouldn't deal with them."

I scoffed at this point. "Really? And now you are some kind of fucking psychologist to tell me what kind of people are suitable for me; Give me a fucking break Alexandros, we're just talking here, sharing a drink; it's not like we're five minutes away from fucking."

With my attempts at appeasing Alexandros' anger, he seemed even more pissed off, as if those Dutch men had harmed him in the nastiest way and I knew nothing about it. To me it seemed ridiculous the way he reacted as I could not find any real grounds for it in my imagination.

"I don't know what has gotten into you, but I urge you to stop before you ruin everything; I don't like the way you're looking at me right now. Put that hatred away now!"

After I added those words, I could see how Alexandros was on the brink of shedding a tear, of anger of course, not sorrow.

Some people cry when they are angry for some reason. I was never able to pull such a stunt.

"Mike, look at me, please … if you love me, you will trust me, and you'll not talk to those men anymore; it's for your own good."

Now I really started to become suspicious as I could feel that Alexandros was not telling me the whole truth. I hated when this type of shit happened, as people expected me to follow them without me knowing a fucking thing about what was really going on; you know, just to follow them in the 'dark' just because they expected it. Fuck that; if I was more inquisitive than anyone believed me to be … that was their misfortune.

"What the fuck is going on?" I growled at him. "Do you know them or some shit?"

Right when I asked Bruno. He smiled and raised his hand. "Could we have another round, please Alexandros?"

His smile was fucking contagious, but then it hit me … how the fuck did he know the name of the 'bartender'? They said that it was their first time to the island and yet they felt so familiar. A million thoughts crossed through my mind and a million scenarios competed against each other … but then I imagined that they must have heard someone calling Alexandros and they remembered. It's not that unusual, you know, it happens all the time.

Alexandros tuned his head towards them and he nodded with a smile, letting them know that the drink was 'on the way'. His smile turned into an icy expression as soon as he turned back to face me. Alexandros' swag was completely gone now as I waited for my explanation.

"I gotta go … I gotta get those drinks." He mumbled as he tried to flee the scene.

Bad luck for him, as I had no intention to let him slip through my grip so easily. I wanted an explanation and I was going to have it … and I wanted to hear it from his mouth.

"You ain't going anywhere, mister … not before I get my explanation!"

He blinked a few times, as if he tried to pick the best explanation out of a row of many.

"No, I haven't seen them in my life. Are you happy now? Can I go?"

His words did not sound convincing at all, but I did not have any other way to block him, especially since again, the Dutch men had told me that it was their first trip to Mykonos. I was left with a bitter taste in my mouth about the whole situation, as I felt that there was something fishy in the air.

I did not want to damage things too much between Alexandros and I, so I let him go; contradictory thoughts bugged me, and I realized that I shouldn't have been so rough on him. I knew I had been mistaken, but the deed was done now! That next morning, I knew I would have a storm brewing and I had to deal with it, one way or another.

"Thank you so much!" I replied with a cynic voice.

I don't know why I did it, I guess it was an uncontrolled re-action caused by the presence of the Dutch fellows. I guess I tried without even noticing to make an impression on them or something.

The sudden blush caused by Alexandros' presence faded away in seconds as soon as he was gone. I was back in business, so to speak and our discussions advanced … Bruno and Daan were really nice guys, 'slightly' older than me … if fifteen years can be called slightly. Nonetheless, their physical shape was one to envy for their bodies were tall and lean, slim fit, just like any man would like to be in his later forties.

At one point as Maria of Carlos Santana started to bounce in the speakers, we all went to the dance floor. This was a jam to die for, and I just could not keep my feet still while the speakers blasted fire through the club.

Bruno and Daan were fairly good dancers too; I gotta admit they took me by surprise considering their age and height. I took them for old schoolers at first as they got their moves going …

We rubbed our asses against one another in that slow jam. It felt fucking surreal to see I was having such a good time with guys who were practically strangers. That was not so unusual for me, as I am outgoing and can make friends easily, but I had never met men who partied like these Dutch guys before; I guess they were the exception this time, ha-ha.

An hour into Alexandros finishing his shift, the flying Dutchmen left Mykonian City pub with a promise to return the next evening so that we could have some more good times together. We hugged as they left, and then I returned to my private corner to wait for my lover. Slightly past five a.m. I could not see my Greek boy. Alexandros was nowhere to be found, and that caused me to believe that he had already left … you know, as he was mad about my little 'endeavour'.

The previous night he had become angry because some stranger wanted to dance with me; now he could not suffer seeing me even talking with those Dutch men. It looked as if I headed for a damn rollercoaster ride with Alexandros.

I decided to wait for a little bit, as I hoped he would pop up, but he failed to do so. I grew more and more impatient and I just wanted to bust in the back and get my hands on him. As luck would have it, I did not have to apply such drastic measures; Alexandros came out into the light to serve a table in the opposite corner of the club.

"There you are!" I mumbled to myself and I went for the ambush.

As he returned and wanted to get behind the bar, I jumped in front of him, somewhat out of nowhere, and that kinda startled him … a little bit.

"Where do you think you are going mister?"

Alexandros turned his face away from me and he tried to go around me; there was no way I was going to let him slide by so easily.

"I am talking to you! I know you can hear me!"

I insisted and I even grabbed his right arm at this point. I could feel the tension and the anger in his muscles. Surely it was not a good sign for me, but I was determined to appease him one way or another.

"Aren't you busy anymore?" I asked.

He ground his teeth. "I got stuff to do …"

The grudge in his voice was obvious; there was friction between us now; alas it was not the good kind.

Needless to say, I could not make too much of a fuss at that point. Alexandros was determined to go, and truth be said, he also needed to take care of the chores before his shift ended. I was not going to be absurd about it and I let him go as I did not want to cause a scandal at the break of dawn.

"Hey, please don't be like that … I will explain everything to you when we go home."

He didn't even blink. He only looked at me with an angry vibe in his eyes.

"I am going now!"

The grinding of his teeth gave me Goosebumps; I let go of his hand and I returned to my corner. I looked at him as he disappeared behind the bar, and I wondered what this man wanted from me. I could not live the secluded life of a monk just because we were sort of together. I mean, I had to interact with other people too, and I could not understand why he perceived everything to be so 'sexual'. Only time would tell how things between us would unfold.

Sensual Churaga

We did leave together that morning, but Alexandros was kinda on strike. He refused to talk to me too much and he would only say the basics when he needed something. It was clear to me that I had no chance to get more out of him and I decided to let it slide … that one instance at least.

This was the second day I spent on Mykonos and still no sex; I didn't know why but it looked like I had caught Alexandros on the bad side this year. Something was going on with him, but I was clueless about what was to be revealed fairly soon.

After a little bit of innocent foreplay and spooning, both Alexandros and I fell asleep in each other's arms. Neither of us came, … and that was because we did not even try jerking off or blowing. I don't know, I just think the overall mood killed any sexual drive. So, you can see it is not all about the dick and ass; … the brain had a lot to do in this game and if your mind is fucked up from all the bickering, yes … you just can't fucking do a thing.

I hoped that the waters between Alexandros and I would soon clear up and that we would start to have a really good time. Remembering the previous year, I just could not imagine how we hadn't broken a few beds already.

A surprise was in order for him. As we woke up, I told him to get ready as it was beach time; a quick scooter ride and we were at Churaga Beach. This was a cute but fancy destination for all who wanted to get a good tan and eat the best food.

'Our Tavern' was right next to the beach and we called it that as we spent most of our time there. The Ouzo they served there was the most hilarious I have ever tasted in my life … a funny drink if you ask me, but one that will fuck you up really quick if you got a bit reckless with it.

As we settled at a table, I could feel that Alexandros was still stressed out; my intention was to get him to unwind a bit, but it looked like he had something else on his mind … and it bothered him quite a bit.

The scenery was perfect; the sun shone through the few scattered clouds and the breeze felt just perfect on my skin. I figured a quick harmless question could not hurt him in these conditions … so I went for it.

"What is going on Alexandros? What's bothering you?"

He sighed, and looked at his hands resting in his lap.

"I don't know Mike; something does not feel right. What are we doing here?"

This chain of thoughts he put on the table kinda got me stranded. 'What did he mean,' I thought. It was all devoid of sense, his question I mean. It was pretty obvious to me.

"We're having a good time?" I mumbled as my right eyebrow shot up. "The weather is perfect, we're here … the food is great …"

Alexandros shook his head; disappointment and fear lurked under his skin; his eyes did not lie and not they were not even trying to, but I was unaware of his deeper fears.

"Not here, at the tavern … US!" he stressed. "What's to become of us? We have fun one or two weeks during the summer and then what? What sort of relationship is this? Where are we going with it?"

Indeed, his claims were as valid as the fucking air I breathed, but I guess I was not ready to face them. I had come to Mykonos to meet him and to have a good time, and I was now faced with serious life choices and a decision that I was not ready to take yet.

"But … hold on for a moment, I thought we agreed about this …"

I mumbled those words, and at that very moment they made no sense to me. I am sure he did not understand a fucking thing either … or did he …?

"Agreed on what?"

He lashed out at me more viciously this time.

"I see you dancing with all sorts of men, you talk, and you share drinks while I bust my ass behind the bar. That's not fair, you know. I mean, I can see your movements and you don't seem to care at all if you rub your dick against others."

This was a fucking avalanche of jealous accusations coming my way, and there was no way for me to dodge it. All I could do was stand my ground and try to face it the best way I could. Alexandros' uncertainties and fears of losing me were all slowly surfacing now. I guess he had not had the courage to say it to my face up to that point, or maybe he had struggled to find the perfect moment.

I have no idea what the actual cause was, but one thing was crystal clear now; I had an aching lover on my hands, and I had to deal with his drama one way or another. I had to act smooth.

"But I thought you loved working at the bar?" I argued, but he kept shaking his head.

"I am sick of that place; I am sick of this island … I am sick of it all!" He cried out and now I found myself out in the open, with nothing to link with to make him calm down. Thus, he continued with his bickering …

"I wanna get out of this forsaken island. I have had enough of it already, I don't even feel alive anymore; fixing drinks for bored clients is not the lifestyle for me, I was not born to waste my life in this manner."

Angry as Alexandros was at that point, he called the waiter and he asked for some Ouzo. I just sat there on the opposite side of the table and I looked at him without being able to utter a word. My mind was overworked as I tried to find a solution to take him out of that dark state. I unfortunately could not find any answer as his manifestation came out of the blue and I had had no idea that he really felt that way, up to that moment.

"I think I will leave Greece this year." He mumbled and chugged the glass of Ouzo.

"And go where?"

My eyes were foggy at this point; I could not look at him as a matter of fact I was not looking at anything. I was staring into an invisible abyss that only I could see.

"I don't know." He added, "The UK maybe … a lot of people are going there, it seems like life is good down there."

I shrugged; I did not find myself in any position to counsel him in any way. Heck, I had travelled and lived in various countries myself, since an early age. I could not tell him not to leave Mykonos, as I would look like a hypocrite and that was the last thing, I wanted to happen that day.

Of course I felt somewhat egoistic in my thoughts as I would miss him if he left the island, but it wasn't egoistic to ask a man to sacrifice his life and happiness for me. If he felt miserable there, then it was his right to search for his own happiness wherever destiny would take him.

"Maybe I can come with you … hmm … doesn't that sound like a great idea? That we can always be together, not just during a few short weeks during summer."

Well, that thought caught me mid-air … and without a parachute at that. I had not thought that Alexandros would go that far. I mean, I didn't dislike that idea from the start, but it felt a little bit too much and too sudden. The truth was, I didn't want to upset him either, so I just kept my mouth shut and I sipped from my glass, hoping that this urge of his would soon fade away.

Alas, that did not happen, and Alexandros insisted as if he begged for an answer from me.

"So, what do you think? Doesn't that sound like a great idea?"

I fucking choked on my drink, and I even spilled some of it down on my pristine white shirt.

"Shit!" I ground my teeth in my futile attempt to clear the stain with my bare hand. "You were saying?" I mumbled.

I looked at him, as I struggled not to make any gesture that would seem too dubious.

"The moving ... with you."

His face had turned so calm now and his dark brown eyes shone against the burning sun; damn he looked like he had just had an epiphany and I just sat there without an answer. Alexandros' sudden serenity fucking scared me now ... and that was because I knew that my answers would be wrong, regardless of what I would choose to say. For that reason, I decided to go smooth on him.

"Yeah, that sounds like a promising perspective."

My voice was as soft as it could get, yet my hands fucking shook; luckily, I had them under the table and that meant that he could not see them.

"Doesn't it ... I would quit and fucking move tomorrow." He added in a cheerful voice and at that point my heart started to race like a fucking stallion.

I could not see but I could feel the stressed grimace on my face; these things you can't control as much as you want to, and they tend to give up your actual thoughts and your intentions.

There I sat, defenceless in front of the man who was the closest ever, to having the keys to my heart. I still had mixed thoughts as I had always kept my options open, and I did not like to feel trapped in the arms of a single man ...

The feeling was a bit strange, as I did not want to lose him either; yes, I might sound like a bitch right now, but that's how I felt. I wanted to live life and taste from every delicious dish possible.

"Don't you think you are rushing it a little bit right now. We have good days and bad days. You don't need to change the fucking continent just because someone upset you at work one day."

A wide smile from ear to ear covered my face as I uttered those words. I thought that this would calm down his enthusiasm at least just for a bit. Alexandros was unfortunately fired up already as he planned our life together before I could say a fucking word.

"You know how I hate it when other men hit on you … how will I know what you are doing back home when I am not with you."

Ohh shit! That was too sensitive. I could not believe he had gone that far with his controlling. I had to stand up for myself.

"Hold on for a minute. What is it that you are implying, huh? That I will be fucking every living thing after I leave Mykonos. I don't think you should judge me, as I did not judge you. I don't believe that you would wear a chastity belt for the rest of the year when I am away from you. Please don't be a hypocrite Alexandros, it doesn't suit you well!"

I had to lash out at Alexandros. He had to know his place; after all we were not married or anything. I did not like it when he acted like a freak, by accusing me of being unfaithful and all that shit.

"Don't you understand it pains me to know that some other man is touching you … I simply can't control that feeling," he replied in a sorrowful voice; but I did not buy it at all.

"Stop it right there!" I warned him. "Otherwise you will ruin everything with your paranoia."

A deep silence came upon us; it felt as if we had forgotten how to speak all of a sudden and it was strange. Just like two strangers of different tongues who just happened to end up at the same table. We sat there looking in different directions, each thinking of his own problems. The thing was, we both shared the same problem now, but we were looked at it from different perspectives and that made a big difference.

It didn't take two minutes, and Alexandros stood up from his seat; restless as he looked for his scooter.

"I have to go …," he muttered, without even looking at me. His voice was slightly nervous.

'Right now,' I wondered. "We are barely here, and we haven't even got to the beach yet. What's the rush?"

He shook his head as he muttered some gibberish that I could not understand.

"I gotta go… I remembered I have something to take care of soon."

"You're sure that you can't stay for a little longer? There's still enough time until you have to start your shift."

I insisted, and hoped that I could convince him to stay, but Alexandros' mind was made up already and it looked as if I had no chance to make him change his mind.

"It's not about work, it's something else." He added one step out of the tavern terrace already.

I looked at his rushed movements with a dazzled eye. "Talk to you tonight, then?"

He had his back to me already and he kept shaking his head. "Yeah, sure, whatever ...," he muttered or at least that's what I think he said.

Alexandros hopped on his scooter and he faded away in the distance. I was left there at the tavern with a million thoughts on my mind and uncertainty of what was to happen next. Alexandros wanted a full commitment, yet I had no idea if I was supposed to provide such a thing while he ... did whatever he wanted.

Frankly, I hadn't stuck my nose into his business for over the year and that was not because I didn't care what he did or with whom he did it with while I was back on the continent. It was his private business as well as mine was mine and I felt that I should not have to explain myself for the choices I made.

At that point, my appetite was gone along with my will to relax on the beach. I gazed at the waves for a while as they crashed on the shore, and then I decided that it was not worth it. I found no pleasure in doing anything alone.

As a result, I left to back to my hotel room, alone and disappointed about my quarrel with Alexandros. On my way back I struggled to understand why people couldn't just enjoy life without all the useless complication.

It was a mystery to me how we tended to ruin everything just for the sake of doing it. In any case, I hoped that Alexandros would chill out during the rest of the day and that he would show a different face later that night at the club.

The hours until the evening that day passed as if they were grinding against the earth; it's almost excruciating how time tends to fuck with you in your worst moments. It's like someone or something tries to prologue your pain by stretching each second to its limits.

I can tell you I had a lot of time to think about Alexandros and our future together if there was to be one. Those long hours that seemed to never end, allowed me to realize that fighting comes always from too much passion and pathos invested in a relationship … at least that happens in most cases. The resolution I came up with was that I had to give 'us' a second chance. Therefore, I dressed myself in the fanciest clothes I had, poured a ton of perfume on my skin … hoping to catch his attention at the club and maybe appease his aching heart some way; only God knew.

The fucking mirror sparkled; those tight blue pants like the sea sat tightly on my ass and the dark beige t-shirt was filling the picture perfectly. My feet were shod with a pair of dark brown moccasins, perfectly matched to the shirt. My hair was flung back as if it had been blown by the most powerful wind.

This was an outfit to die for; I knew it and I knew its effects. All I could hope for now was to catch the right prey, as more often than not, when I tried to impress someone, I ended up with ten others queuing behind my back, trying their luck.

When I finally reached Mykonian City pub, at around eight-forty p.m., I could see that the place was already packed. My corner was reserved already as I made way through the crown, I could feel how heads turned behind me, and someone even dared to tap my ass quickly. I could not tell who that was, but I didn't bother too much about it, as it was not the first time it had happened.

Alexandros picked up my presence first, as I got closer to the bar. I obviously wanted to say, 'Hi,' but when he saw me as I came closer he pretended to be busy and tried to flee the scene. Too bad, that was not his lucky moment; I had gotten to the club with one thought in mind and that was exactly what I was gonna do.

"Hey handsome, where do you think you are going?" I almost yelled at him.

Again, he tried to act as if he did not hear me, but I knew he did.

"Come here!" I added in a bossy voice and luckily, he submitted to my will.

"Hey, what's up?" he mumbled in a distant voice.

He seemed preoccupied and slightly embarrassed about what he had done earlier that day.

"You feeling all right? Did you take care of your business?" I asked him, but he seemed rather absent minded.

"Ugh … yeah, sure, everything is in perfect order now."

For a second it crossed my mind that he just made up the reason to leave the tavern and even now I am not a hundred percent sure that he had not lied, but that's another story.

"I am glad to hear that. Shall I buy you a drink or something?"

He refused to answer, and I couldn't see why; that was not the first time I had offered him a drink. He worked at a club after all. It wasn't that he was not allowed to have one or two during the night.

"No thanks, I'm good," he said, and with those words our talking was done.

I did not insist anymore but it looked like it was a bad omen. I say this as my Dutch boys did not show up that night and at one point the whole island ran out of power for some reason. We just sat there in the dark almost, with no music, a fact that bored me to death. All the alcohol in the world could not improve the situation. With nothing else to do, I decided to flee the scene and relax for the rest of the night; but not before I spoke to Alexandros. You see, we still had some unfinished business and I wanted to talk to him, seriously this time.

I caught him as he passed by, and I grabbed his hand to pull him over. Surprisingly, he did not fight back, and he almost landed in my lap.

"I want to see you when your shift ends," I whispered into his ear.

He nodded. Almost too easy, if you ask me.

"I will leave my door open so you can come straight in," I added.

A smile met me from his side; I was taken back for a moment.

"I will see you there … now I have to go. I have a ton of work to complete," he said.

"Okay," I mumbled. "See you then."

It was around four a.m. when I finally reached my hotel room. I still felt restless and I could not close an eye. I don't know why, but something felt as if it were missing that morning. I couldn't find peace, no matter what I tried to do.

It did not take me long until I logged in on Grindr. Yeah, we all know that gay app that promises to give us the best but doesn't always do it. Anyway, I did not plan on meeting anyone that night; my only intention was to ask for a pic or two, so that I could rub one out a little better.

As I swiped left and right, I guess Alexandros or some of his friends saw me online. That is the perk of it, people can see you when you are on, and I guess he assumed that I looked to hook up with someone to fuck.

I am not entirely sure whether Alexandros found out about it or not, but the thing is he never showed up at the hotel that morning. He did not call or text to warn me about anything; he just failed to come … just perfect silence.

I had to now sleep alone, not that it bothered me that much, but I felt a bit betrayed. I kinda started to dislike Alexandros' behavior and his sudden moods.

He acted like a moody teenage girl, and I kinda hated that shit. We were not seventeen-year-olds anymore, and I thought that he understood that too. 'Who knows, maybe he was still transitioning at that point …'

That wank felt dry and kinda forced, but I had to do it; I barely came after a while. All those pictures on the web did not help me, but luckily, I fell asleep eventually. I can't tell exactly when that happened but thank God I did not struggle anymore. For a few hours I was off to wonderland, no dream or nightmare, just a peaceful sleep that took over me like a nice tranquil autumn rain.

When I finally opened my eyes, I glanced at the phone and it showed one p.m. Daamnn, that was right in time! I don't know how but a quick thought came to my mind … no Alexandros on the menu for that afternoon. Instead, I quickly searched for Bruno and Daan on Facebook and set a date.

'God bless this technology and social media,' I laughed to myself after the meet up was set at Elia Beach.

If Alexandros kept playing so hard to get with me, then he would get his lesson; I was not going to call or text him for the rest of that day. And later on, at the club, if he continued to act like a bitch, then I would simply ignore his ass until he came to his senses.

Splendid Amalia

In less than half an hour after I spoke to Bruno, my beach body was ready to roll baby. This time I went for a pink t-shirt and white shorts, and a pair of fancy Ray Ban sunglasses. A man's gotta do what a man's gotta do to impress, right?

When I got to my destination, I parked my scooter next to a small tavern that was placed close to the beach itself; Bruno and Daan were already there, for some time I guess and they met me with waves and smiles; it looked as if they were really glad to see me.

"Heey Mike, over here!" Bruno shouted but I had already seen them.

I rushed to the terrace to greet them. "Wassup guys?"

Daan got up from his chair to give me a hug and then Bruno followed seconds later.

"Wassup man, you look like a fucking bomb today."

Bruno's remark made me laugh; literally. I knew my worth but the way he said it, his cheeky attitude made it sound like I had come to rock the party.

"I can say the same thing about you guys … you haven't aged a bit since we last saw each other."

My reply was a bit mean; I was aware of it, but the Dutch folks took my dark humour quite well.

"Ha-ha, you young stallion, you know how to play the game! Come have a seat with us, we were just about to order something to eat ... pizza of the house, sound good for you?"

Daan looked relaxed as he waved at the waiter. A young Greek boy, roughly in his early twenties, dark curly hair, slightly longer, pristine shaved face and smelling of quality perfume as he approached.

"Kalimera!" he said in Greek. "What may I get you."

Daan jumped in and took over. "A large pizza of the house, and drinks for my boys and whatever their hearts desire, for starters."

Bruno shrugged. "I say we should start light with a cocktail each."

I had nothing against that. Cocktails were my favourites anyway, so it was a perfect start for me. The drinks came fairly quickly, but I could not take my eyes and my mind from that handsome looking waiter. I wondered whether he was gay, as his body language told me so; yet, I could not just ask him upfront. I did not want be rude to him or anything. I had my hands full anyway at that time, but you know how that little devil called curiosity stirs you up when you least expect it.

Bruno, Daan, and I ate pizza, drank our cocktails and much more and at one point we started to share things about each other, you know, getting to know each other a bit better. I was curious, I won't deny it; there was something mysterious about these two middle-aged Dutch men that made me want to know more.

That was the moment of truth, so to speak; I was usually rather reluctant about telling people details about my life and the things I went through, but for some reason, I found it comfortable to talk to Bruno and Daan about it. My charismatic smile did hide some pretty nasty shit, and I guess that was the reason I did not like to speak too much about it.

Drama is a little child compared to what I had to go through. The thing is only a year ago, my mother was diagnosed with cancer. That day, I felt like the world was about to end for me.

I almost fucking blacked out. My mother hadn't felt well for a while, but there's something about that cursed news 'she has cancer'. The word cancer rewires your fucking brain for some reason, and I made no exception to that rule.

Bruno grabbed my hand when he heard. "Man I am so sorry. Is there anything we could help you with?"

I wept and went on. "She's better now, but it's been quite a struggle."

My father and I haven't been the best of pals either, since the day I told him I was gay. He rejected me as if I was a fucking leper or something, and he could never make peace with my choices in life. There was nothing I could do about that, but I did not really try; it was not my problem, it was his and he could take it to his grave if that's what he wanted. Then my brother who messed up with my ex-boyfriend; he too broke contact for no good reason.

As for my health, that's been a rollercoaster too; with heart failure and a recent break up from the love of my life as I had messed around. It was totally my fault and I would never forgive myself for that. I don't know if the heart failure was a direct consequence of the pain I felt or not, but I am sure that it was linked in some twisted way.

A life full of bouncing from ecstasy to agony; I am not complaining, because I love life and I try to live and enjoy every bit of it, with all its exoticism and drama. It could not really be called life if all went smoothly and perfectly, am I right? There must be some turmoil inserted here and there.

As I finished telling them about my life, Bruno, and Daan gazed at me with a look in their eyes as if they could not believe it.

"Damn, that's worthy of a book," Daan added, and that remark made me smile.

Bruno laughed straight up, with his contagious laughter that always pushed me to laugh too.

"Sure thing, you'd be a fool not doing so."

"Yeah, I guess, I'll think about it."

Daan, on the other hand was a married man of thirteen years who had been through a divorce six years before. The whole process took its toll on him, but he had recovered stronger than before; he and his husband just could not work things out anymore and decided to split … better that way. One thing I learned myself too, you just cannot force love into happening. He was a successful businessman though, and he owned a castle in central Netherlands, which was a sign that divorce did not take him down; I guess his black humour and exquisite sarcasm helped me get through the hardships of my life.

Bruno also had a story worth remembering; he told me how he had 'helped' a female friend conceive a child as she could not find a decent man. He wanted a child but did not want to marry a woman, so that's how their baby boy, Tobias who was fifteen months old, came into the world.

Incredible life stories about incredible men, that was without a doubt. I loved to listen to them talk, especially when Bruno started to laugh; this man was one of a kind and I just could not help but laugh whenever he said something funny and laughed about it … it was magnetic in a way, I had to laugh.

Anyway, as we enjoyed our drinks and pizza, I heard my phone ringing, and when I picked it up, I saw that it was Alexandros.

"Fuck you!" I mumbled to myself and I shoved the phone back into my pocket. I was ready to get back to our engrossing conversation when the phone started to ring again.

"Goddamn it!" I ground my teeth and squeezed the phone with my right hand.

Bruno and Daan noticed that I had become restless, so they stopped talking.

"Is everything okay?" Daan asked and I tried to pretend that everything was cool … but what use was it to lie to them?

"A friend of mine keeps calling me. I don't know what the hell he wants that he insists so much. Can't he just understand that I am busy, and he should call me some other time?"

Bruno put up a kind smile. "Why don't you answer? Maybe it's something serious and he needs your help right now; you can never tell. Call him back and see what's going on."

I had second thoughts to call Alexandros back, and that's because I did not want to hear his hysterical voice. My train of thought was suddenly interrupted when the phone started to ring again, the third time now; that was the point where I got up from my chair and took a few steps away from the table … for a little bit of privacy, of course. I pushed the button and answered angrily.

"What the hell do you want? Didn't you get it that I did not want to talk to you if I didn't answer the first time?"

Alexandros didn't even hear my words, or at least he did not care … as he started to interrogate my ass the next second.

"Where are you?"

His voice was agitated at this point.

"Why should you care?" I replied ironically. "I am where I wanna be … I am a grown man. I don't have to explain myself to you."

"Mike, this is not a joke … tell me you are not with those Dutch men, please."

Alexandros' obsession with Bruno and Daan had started to drive me crazy; my hair literally stood up on my head, and I started to yell at him without even realizing it.

"Listen here, you little brat. I am sick of your jealous games, okay? I came here to have a good time and enjoy my vacation; if you think you can ruin that for me with your petty crisis, then you have another thing coming."

"Please get away from them …" he insisted with the same stupid phrase.

"And why should I do that, huh? They are two wonderful gentlemen and I am having a great time with them; stop acting like a jealous little bitch and mind your own business. I waited for you in the morning, but it looks like you had more important business to take care of. Now suck it up and let me enjoy myself."

"You don't know them …" he whined again, but I couldn't care less.

"And neither do you, since you said you never met them before." I lashed out at him. "Stop being so paranoid and let me be, bye!"

I closed up on him before Alexandros could say another word and with a satisfied look on my face too. I had taught that son of a bitch the lesson he deserved. I wasn't going to let anyone ruin my day. I felt too fabulous, fuck that.

I returned to Bruno and Daan, with a wide smile from ear to ear.

"Everything okay?" Bruno asked and I just nodded my head with confidence.

"Fucking perfect, I would say ... just a mild disturbance but it won't happen again."

Daan seemed fairly ecstatic about the news and he ordered another round of cocktails for the three of us. I was fired up by now and when that sexy looking waiter returned, I felt as if I had to do my game a little bit. I called the guy to my side and I whispered something into his ear ... what do you think it was, huh?

"I think I like you." I said to him with the sexiest damn voice I could muster.

The young lad blushed instantly and gave me that 'fuck me' look. We all know that look, regardless if it's about men or women. We all have it and it's too damn obvious to ignore it.

Bruno did not ignore it either. As soon the boy was gone, he leaned over the rustic wooden table with a smirk on his face.

"Looks like you've gotten yourself some action for today." He grinned but I just waved my hand through the air.

I was laid back at that moment, I smiled. "Nah, I was just fucking with him, just to see how he would react."

"We all know those 'fuck me' eyes," Daan added with a smirk and now I doubted it myself.

After we had some more drinks at the tavern, we headed to the Mykonian Beach Club; that was an exquisite location just by the beach where Conchita, the famous Drag Queen of Mykonos sang twice a week. We only learned after we arrived that it was the owner's birthday, so you can imagine that it was a show to remember ... with a fireworks show at the end as the final surprise.

Bruno, Daan and I had a fucking blast down at the beach; we danced and drank only the best the host had to offer and the day was barely half over; I mean, we would certainly be meeting at Mykonian City pub for more partying and drinking in the night.

The show was over around ten-thirty p.m., and I swear I wished that it would last forever; it was so amazing that I felt that I did not want to leave that beach for another twenty-four hours.

Bruno came to me when we left as we left Mykonian Beach Club separately. Each of us needed to go home, take a shower, eat something, and then change clothes so that we could hit Mykonian City pub fresh and ready for another round.

"We'll meet you there, right? At the bar?" he said.

I nodded with certainty; yet there was a certain eagerness about Bruno's voice as if he HAD to see me at the Mykonian City pub. We were kinda holiday friends now, but I could not have imagined that they couldn't spend a night without me … it would not be the first one anyway.

"Sure thing, I'll be there …" I smiled, "I would not miss it for the world!"

Bruno grinned … again. "Good, Good, I'll see you there, don't miss it."

I smiled too and left. At first I did not think too much about it, but as I got back to the hotel and I got under the hot water of the shower, questions started to pop up in my head. First, about why Alexandros was so agitated about these two middle-aged men who appeared to be harmless and about their kindness to me. These two things did not agree with one another, and for some reason I got Goosebumps even while the hot water poured over me.

Confused and slightly dizzy, I stepped out of the shower in a rush; the hotel room felt cold now that the steam was gone. I started to feel chilly and I dug through the white wooden closet for a t-shirt or something, as I felt as if I was going to freeze to death. It was unclear whether the weather was to blame or if it was the effect of all those unanswered questions.

Eventually, I found a light green V necked t-shirt, one that I kinda detested but I always took it with me on my trips for some reason; at that moment I did not have time to be too picky, so I put it on. I picked a pair of white sexy Kelvin Klein boxers and I returned to the bathroom to fix myself a bit. My hair was kinda mushy now after that hot shower and there was no way in the world that I would be able to face myself at the club if I looked like that. I had to look impeccable otherwise I would not leave the fucking room, I swore to God.

I brushed my teeth and combed my hair. At that point, my eyes stared straight into the mirror as if I looked into the eyes of a ghost. I wondered what the night would bring, but most importantly, I tried to find an answer as to why I started to feel so 'funny', and by funny I mean distressed.

My stare was fruitless; I could not reach any conclusion, but at the same time, I knew that I would meet Alexandros at Mykonian City pub that night and that he would give me some answers, or else I would slap the shit out of him, in front of everyone at the bar … I did not give a fuck.

That night I tried a more exotic outfit. I got dressed in a green neck black shirt, accompanied by a grey blazer and a pair of dark brown tight pants. I wanted my ass to lash out … after such a splendid day I knew I deserved such a treat. When I walked out of the door, I think the clock hit around eleven-thirty p.m. and the breeze of the Aegean hit me right in my perfect hair. For some reason, the moon was exceptionally beautiful that night, all full and bright, you'd say it was almost daylight.

The perfect scenery if you ask me. It unfortunately foretold nothing of what was to happen later. Needless to say, I set off for the club with the best intentions; but as soon as I reached the club and entered the building, my eyes were drawn towards something I did not expect. I had expected that Bruno and Daan would be there, but never in a million years did I imagine that I would find them nose to nose with Alexandros, right by the bar, as if they had some sort of fucking business to settle.

I was awestruck for a moment, but it did not take me long to recover from my dazzled state. I tucked up my sleeves and I burst onto the scene to find out what the hell was going on; surely someone would have some answers for me.

"Well, hello, hello ladies. What do we have here? Some sort of meet-up I wasn't aware of?"

My sarcasm pierced through the loud music of the club like a well sharpened dagger. In a split second, both Bruno and Daan turned their faces towards me, and I could not help but notice their surprised look. Alexandros, on the other hand, looked rather panicked and he tried to hide his face from me.

"Ohh, you're here already?" Bruno said with a cheerful voice that was nothing but a failed attempt to hide his anxiety.

"Looks like I am. Did you already see me as I saw you from a mile away."

My comment stirred laughter in Bruno, but that was not my intention and I did not laugh as I normally would at his laughter. I felt rather angry at that time, and my eyes were riveted on Alexandros' hands as he tried to hide them behind his back. He didn't greet me and he looked like he was on the point of leaving through the back door, without even saying a goddamn word to me. I could not leave things like this, so I pushed Bruno and Daan aside so that I could reach Alexandros to have a word or two with him.

"If you can excuse me …," he blurted as I ground my teeth and made my way towards him. "What?" Alexandros eventually muttered.

I grabbed his ass and I pulled it towards the stairs that lead to the bathroom.

"No, no, no, don't give me that innocent look. What are you doing with them? You desperately called me to tell me to get away from them and now you are talking to them as if you are friends or some shit. What the fuck is going on here, Alexandros? You'd better tell me the truth otherwise; I will lose my shit."

My expression was tense and fucking wrinkled from all the nerves and anger; my grip was tight on his arm, but Alexandros didn't even flinch and he avoided my eyes.

"I'm talking to you, goddamn it! Are you going to tell me what the hell is going on here?"

"I can't … I can't do it here, it's too dangerous, I'm sorry."

His eyes were fixed on Bruno and Daan as he said those words and I felt bound to turn my head and take another look at those two Dutch men; they seemed harmless to me.

"What the fuck are you talking about man? This is not the hood, it's Mykonian City pub. What danger are you talking about?

I lashed out at Alexandros, but he refused to talk to me. At the same time, he kept his hands hidden behind his back as if he tried to conceal something from me. I was at my wits end at that point.

I think I lost it for a second and I started to shake the shit out of Alexandros, saying, "I told you I wasn't fucking around."

It is quite unclear to me how or what had happened, but Alexandros dropped something on the floor of the club that moment, and he dived like a fucking scuba diver to grab that shit … it was as if his very existence depended on him holding onto it.

'Is that fucking insulin or what?' I thought to myself for a split second, but I could not be farther from the truth, boy!

"Leave me alone, you've caused me enough problems already… I tried to protect you!" Alexandros almost shouted those words to me and I backed off.

"Protect me? From the devil or who the fuck?" I yelled back and then he nodded his head towards Bruno and Daan who were already leaving the club for some reason.

"Goddamn it … get your ass in here!"

I grabbed Alexandros' arms tightly and I pulled him inside the bathroom; I blocked the door behind us with a garbage bin, then I pushed him against the sinks.

"If you're not gonna tell me what the hell is going on, RIGHT GODDAMN NOW, I swear to God I'll smash your head against the sink!"

Alexandros sobbed and he dropped the little bag on the floor.

"What the fuck is that you are hiding from me, huh? What is it?"

He burst into tears; his voice was gibberish so I could barely understand what he was saying.

"Coke man … it's coke."

At first, I thought my hearing had failed me, and I heard something else.

"Drugs? At Mykonian City pub? Are you kidding me?"

Alexandros' head shook left and right and the tears had become thicker now.

"Yes, drugs … you caught me. What the fuck do you want from me now? That's the truth, the only one … a few grams worth hundreds of Euros."

I found myself in disbelief as he confessed the truth to me. I never imagined that Alexandros could be capable of such a thing. My Alexandros a fucking drug dealer? My hands shook terribly due to anxiety and anger, and I felt as if I should slap him at least a few times. And that's what I did until I managed to release at least some of that tension.

"What the hell were you thinking? Dealing drugs inside the club? Do you have any idea how dangerous that can be? You could end up spending precious years of your life in jail, and for what? A few paper bills?"

He scoffed. "A few? You have no idea how much money goes around in this business … I would have to work a full year to make what I would selling coke in a week."

I almost pulled out a handful of my hair from my head. "Goddamn it, Alexandros … have you lost your mind? And who the hell is providing you with the coke in the first place?"

"I told you that those Dutch men are dangerous …" He sighed, "They might look harmless to you, but you have no idea what their real intentions are."

You can imagine I was in shock. "Bruno and Daan? Are you kidding with me? They're like the nicest people I've met in my life."

"Appearances can be deceiving Mike … you shouldn't trust people so easily." Alexandros added and I felt really hurt and betrayed.

"Yeah? Like I have trusted you with my whole heart?"

Alexandros fell onto his knees on the cold marble floor; he grabbed the coke bag and he threw it inside the closet; his voice now sounded tired and mostly disappointed in himself.

"I did it … I did it for you; I wanted to leave this cursed place and be with you, but I did not want to be a burden on your back. Life's costs go beyond love, I am too aware of that."

"That's no excuse, Alexandros … poisoning people's lives is not something to joke about or make money from. It's not right."

I blasted him, but he was clearly in another place now and had regretted his deeds.

His breath had become heavy, but not heavier than mine as I was now worried that he used the coke too, and that would be a whole other problem.

"Did you use any?" I asked him with a worried voice. "Alexandros, did you use the coke?"

"No, no, I only sold it to customers. That's all I did, and I took a small part of the money ... I swear to God!"

"Look me in the eyes and swear on your mother's grave that you're not a junky."

At that point, Alexandros' tears intensified. He cried rivers almost on his knees, but I did not feel any pity or mercy for him. I felt betrayed and that was the worst thing for me.

"You can do many other things and I may forgive you for those, but betrayal is something I cannot close my eyes to and pretend it's not there."

"I swear on anything you want ... I did not use it; I was so stupid to even sell it for them, but I did it so that I could be with you."

In a way, I felt as if he had put all his blame on my shoulders as if I had forced him to sell drugs. I felt disgusted as I looked down at him.

"Stop it right there ... don't get me involved in your dirty business because I had nothing to do with it."

Alexandros tried to say something else, but I stopped him; I was at my wits end and I did not want to hear another word.

"You know what?" I ground my teeth. "You can do whatever the fuck you wanna do, Alexandros. I am out of here; I am sick of your shit already, with all your lying, hiding, and shit. I thought you were another kind of man and I actually believed you when you said you loved me. I am out, and please don't follow me."

His face suddenly became pale, but he could not say a word in reply; it was better that way, because it cut me out of all the unnecessary drama.

"You must never look for me from now on! We're done!" I growled at him with all the anger I could muster.

In a split second, I turned around and I walked out of that bathroom with my head held high. I had all the reasons to walk away; after all, I had my pride and that mattered to me.

Alexandros cried his heart out as I closed the door behind me. I could still hear him a few more feet, but I could not go back to him. My heart ached. In spite of all my anger, I did have true feelings for the Greek fool; too bad he disappointed me.

Mykonian City pub was still packed at that time; I think it was half past midnight. People danced under the spotlights. Drinks were served, and it looked as if nothing wrong had happened. In that moment it hit me; we all live our lives in separate bubbles and while some might cry and suffer, others could give less of a fuck. That's how life works after all; a complete and utter twisted randomness if you ask me.

Those bitter tears Alexandros had shed crushed my mood; I could not party anymore, much as I wanted to. The vibe was fucked up now, I had to go. Those 'lovely' Dutch men were long gone when I walked out of that bathroom, so I had no chance to confront them. Right now, my game had stalled, and I had no opponent to face … I just needed to be alone! That was the only way to bring some peace to my heart.

That night, I didn't even get to have one drink because of Alexandros and his devious links with the Dutch; I needed a drink so much … you know, just like a starving bee needs nectar. Before leaving, I went to the bar and I bought a bottle of whiskey; I was going be get fed up, on my own … I was heartily sick of the whole world and its treacheries. With my bottle in my right hand, I walked out of Mykonian City pub and called for a cab; I wanted to get home and open that bottle as soon as possible.

You can imagine that plan did not work too well, as I bust that cap off in the back seat of that cab and I chugged a couple of mouthfuls. At one point, the cab driver figured that he should intervene; he bent his thick grey moustache at me as he showed a bunch of fucked up teeth.

"Wild night huh?" He tried to chuckle but what came out was more like a shitty grimace.

I did not like his intervention! At all! Although a little bit tipsy, I felt as if I should put that nosey stranger in his place.

"Mind your own business and drive this piece of shit; and for the rest of the trip please shut the fuck up, I am trying to think here."

My Gawd, he stared at the whiskey bottle with the scariest eyes I have ever seen when I said I was trying to think. I could see his face in the rearview mirror … that man was terrified. It was hilarious, and for a moment after getting out of the cab, I felt really amused; then I realized that it was no use in being a jerk… but the deed was done now, I could not take my words back.

The atmosphere around the hotel was rather peaceful; no doubt people were out having fun, drinking, and partying and only I had returned around midnight to drink like a lonely bitch.

"What have you done to me, Alexandros …? You fucking jerk, what have you done …?"

Those questions surely had no answers, but I felt bound to shout them out in the air; that gesture brought me a slight sense of relief if I could ever call the way I felt that night relief.

After finally arriving at my room, I dropped my shoes right by the door; the rest of it went right onto the floor in the middle of the room. I quickly grabbed a pair of shorts and then I poured myself another glass. When I looked inside the fridge, I saw I had no ice.

"Goddamn it … this night is going from bad to worse." I cursed, as I ground my teeth. "Damn it, guess I'll be having it dry then."

After hustling around the room for a while and after I emptied close to half of that bottle, boredom started to stretch its long tentacles over me. Mykonian City pub was where all the shit was. Likewise, to stand alone inside the hotel room was the shittiest thing ever; for a moment I figured that I should go back out to a straight club or anywhere else, just to lose that sense of boredom.

That was just a thought that never materialized, because as soon as I went in to have a hot shower, my eyelids started to fall as if they had been shot down or something. With my bathrobe on, I stretched out on the bed and turned the TV on to see what was on, while I thought about where to head next. Yes, that thought was all I got to because I fell asleep before I could find any answers.

A few hours or less, I could not tell for sure how long I was out; the thing is I had a rather troubled sleep, and I guess the fight with Alexandros, and the whiskey had a lot to do with it. I bounced from one state to the other and I think I even opened my eyes in the process as my subconscious tried to decide what needed to be done next. My brain was so fucked up now that it couldn't discern my dreams from reality. I was somewhere in between where everything was shadowy and without substance.

So much so that I did not realize what was going on with me; the soft touches and the kisses went in for quite a while until I understood what was actually happening to me. A dream at first that turned out to be real; when I opened my eyes and rubbed them a few times, I found Alexandros in my room. He undressed me under a rain of kisses and I could not understand what the hell was going on.

"What the fuck? Alexandros, what the hell are you doing here? What time is it?"

My sleepy voice was hardly understandable, but my shock was even greater. Alexandros' shyness was obvious now; he did not reply and he continued to kiss me under my belly button, almost close to kiss my hard cock. I was still confused at this point and I tried my best to wake up. Thus I grabbed his head with both my hands.

"Alexandros, what the fuck are you doing? Stop! What time is it?"

"I don't know, around three a.m.?" His voice stuttered and I could see his scared eyes as he looked at me in a way he never did before.

"What are you doing here?" I asked.

I thought of bashing him again, maybe worse than what had happened at Mykonian City pub, but then I stopped, and I thought again about it. It made no sense to me to make him feel even more miserable. I would try a different tack now.

"Shouldn't you be at work now?" I asked him, but he put his head down as if he did not even hear me and he tried to take my cock into his mouth.

God, that feeling was heavenly. Alexandros knew how to suck a dick! Too bad I was not in the mood for it; the shit was had become too suspicious for my taste and I had to get to the bottom of things. I just couldn't stand to live a lie anymore.

"Stop it, Alexandros, Goddamn it ... answer me. What is going on? Why did you ditch work? Don't tell you did it for me because I am not gonna forgive you for that."

As I finished with my questions, his face turned almost grey with fear; he looked at me but the words failed to come out of his mouth. I knew right then that he had fucked up and that it had nothing to do with our fight.

"What is it?" I insisted and this time he found the power to confess.

"The cops came by Mykonian City pub ... I think they sniffed the drug thing. I had to flee otherwise they would get their hands on me."

"Ohh fuck!" I almost choked. "And you came here ... man I am going home tomorrow. The last thing I need right now is to go to jail because of you. Goddamn it, you had to come here?"

At that point, all my sleepiness had left me at the speed of light. In an instant, I felt as if I had been up for an eternity.

"I'm sorry, I didn't know where to go." He tried to explain. "I don't think they know anything substantial, or that I was involved. You're in no danger!"

I jumped out of the bed and I threw the white coat on the floor. "You don't think? What the fuck is that supposed to mean? You actually have no clue of what the cops know or don't know, and you come to me with empty reassuring words. Please get out of here, before I lose my shit. You've caused me too much trouble thus far ... I am not in the mood for any more of this."

Alexandros clearly did not want to listen to my words; I mean, in his scared state he clearly saw me as his only hope. I felt sorry for him, but I sure as hell did not want to get into trouble for something I didn't even do. I tried to distance myself as quickly as possible, but he fell at my feet, and he literally begged me not to throw him out of my hotel room.

"Please Mike, please believe me I did not want any of this to happen … I just …"

"You just what Alexandros? You thought selling drugs was an easy deal and that you could get away with it. You were reckless to get involved with those Dutch men." My sharp voice pierced through the room like a well sharpened blade and I am sure it went through his heart the same way.

"I know, I know." He sobbed. "You think I don't know … but the pay at the club was so shit. I could not afford anything. I could not build the life I wanted with a few Euros in my pocket. I could not build the life that I wanted with YOU."

"Ohh cut me some slack with that shit! I've heard it too many times already." I lashed out at him and I walked away.

"Mike, please don't go, I beg you." He kept on crying, but I tried to hold my ears closed tight against his cries.

As I approached the window, naked as I was, I could see the police cars driving back and forth with their sirens blaring. That gave me some serious chills down my spine.

"Shit … Alexandros, you are getting me into the deepest shit of my life." I mumbled to myself, but it looked like he heard none of it.

He was right behind me; his hands one on my ass and one on my cock; this little devil knew too well how to play me on his tongue. He started to rub my cock and my butt cheeks until he got the effect he desired. For a moment, I tried to fight back, but it was useless as I loved the way he handled me, so I decided to think less of the consequences and simply enjoy the moment.

Alexandros pushed me against the window, my face towards him this time; then he kneeled in front of me and with a magic twist of his hands he grabbed my cock and gobbled it all down his throat. No gag reflex on this fellow, meaning he could suck a dick … properly!

One hand rubbed my balls while the other explored the vastness of my chest and belly; for a full fifteen minutes Alexandros sucked my dick sending me straight to heaven. It all ended as I came with the load of my life … I guess the stress and the uncertainty had increased the tension of the whole experience.

I almost fell off my feet as he was done with me; a short moment of satisfaction on both sides followed, but the worry came right after. The cops had swarmed around the hotel for some reason, and that fact alone made me restless.

"I am sorry, I caused you so much pain," Alexandros whispered in my ear.

"That might be, but things cannot be undone with a blowjob," I replied, and I went straight for my stroller.

"What are you doing?" he asked me in a confused voice.

"I am leaving, right now. I am in no mood for trouble … I will pay extra for the plane ticket, I don't care, but I am not staying here for another day."

Alexandros' breath stopped for a moment as he gazed at me. He looked as if his brain had rewired right there on the spot, and he waited for the reboot to finish.

"Now?" he eventually muttered with a voice filled with disbelief.

"Yeah, now! I`m not losing another moment. I plan on going home, not to some jail on some godforsaken Greek island."

Alexandros shook his head and he tried to grab my hands. "But you didn't do anything wrong. Why would you get into trouble?"

I was deaf to his arguments at this point; with all the shady shit going on behind my back, only God knew what I had done without even knowing it.

"No Alexandros, I am not going to play your game now; so if you could stay out of my way, that would be great!" as I said those words, I kept on pushing all my mushy clothes into the stroller. The anger in my voice and my movements were obvious, and for that reason, he did not dare to say anything else.

"At least let me help you …," he almost timidly whispered.

I pushed him away. "Please, take your hands off my clothes ... you may stain them with coke or God knows what else. I don't have time for that shit at the airport."

"Okay, okay ... I was just trying to ...," he mumbled.

"Don't try anything right now; you've tried enough and look where that got us."

In less than half an hour I was done with packing and getting dressed; it was four-thirty a.m. and the sun crept up through the feeble clouds in the sky. I was more than ever determined to leave Mykonos, despite having another day to stay. My holiday was fucking ruined now and only trouble would attack me if I stayed here any longer.

I grabbed my stroller and I walked through the door of my room without saying goodbye to Alexandros. I was so tense and angry that I did not even look back; fuck the blowjob, my disappointment was still there ... and that was because I really cared for him, not just for sex. It was much more than that.

Alexandros called my name. "Mike, stop ... please, wait for me!" but I did not flinch. Seconds later, he caught up to me. I could hear his heavy breathing, filled with remorse and pain. "If there's anything I could to ...," he added as he panted with fatigue.

"No!" I murmured without turning my head towards him. "There's nothing you can do right now. You've done already more than was needed to ruin everything. Now leave me alone, I have a plane to catch."

He tried to grab my hand to make me stop, but all his efforts were futile. I pulled my hand back and I continued to walk with the same anger in my steps.

"Take your filthy hands off me!" I said grinding my teeth. "I wish you all the best, you've brought it on yourself!"

At that point, Alexandros stopped following me. He remained petrified behind me and he just looked at how I got away from him. I could see his stone like posture out of the corner of my eye. It was kinda heart-breaking, this scene, but I could not back down, not now; not with all that was at stake.

The keys to my room had remained on the coffee table; I didn't even check out from the hotel as I left. My mind was too caught up with all the troubles I tried to get away from.

I flew through the hotel lobby then out into the street. Alexandros, I believe remained in my room, to fantasize probably at the last remnants of my smell from that day. I could not tell for sure, but frankly I didn't care too much at that time. It take less than five minutes for the taxi to arrive. I got in with my stroller and two words were more than enough.

"Airport please!"

The taxi driver nodded his head and off we went. While I sat in the back seat, I kept having contradictory thoughts about Alexandros and about leaving. I had never had any problems with the law in my life, especially in other countries. We all know what can happen when foreign authorities get their hands on you … especially for some shit you didn't even do.

My mind was troubled, so much so that I didn't even pay attention to the road; the taxi driver seemed professional to me, so I left the paying attention to the road to him. All I wanted now, was to get out of Mykonos as soon as possible; away from Alexandros and all the trouble with the drugs and everything.

My holiday had turned into the nastiest nightmare one I could never have imagined.

I grabbed my phone to check the time, and I thought of turning it off, as I did not want Alexandros to keep calling me while I waited to check in. My head was too heavy to deal with another drama.

Four-fifty-seven a.m.; a time I would never forget in my life; I checked the time with a deep sigh. I didn't even know how I felt anymore. Confused and lonely, maybe disappointed and fatigued … but the pain that followed then was something I would never forget.

I didn't know how or where it came from, but a sudden, violent, and loud 'Bang' assaulted my eardrum. One moment I was in the back seat of the cab, then seconds later, I found myself crawling through twisted metal and broken glass.

The taxi spun a few times on the asphalt and eventually rolled over. It took me a few moments to realize what was going on with me, as it all happened in a flash. Pain and adrenaline rushed in at the same time, in such high doses that I felt as if I was about to have a heart attack.

"Sir, Sir, are you, all right?" I kept asking the taxi driver, but the poor man was gone; he had died instantly on impact.

"Shit!" I ground my teeth and I tried to make out what had happened.

The car was so twisted that I could barely move; luckily, I still had my phone in my hand from the moment I had wanted to turn it off, and the bloody thing still worked. With my last bit of strength, I dialled 112, to call for help, as I had no idea how long I was going to survive inside that twisted wreck.

When they finally picked up the call, a lady said something to me in Greek; I could not understand shit! I presume she asked me what the emergency was, or at least that's what I assumed.

"I am trapped in a taxi; there's been an accident on the way to the airport, the driver is dead."

She kept asking me what road, but I had no fucking clue and I could feel my power slipping away.

"I don't know, I don't know... send someone goddamn it, how many roads go to the airport on this godforsaken island?"

Those were the last things I yelled into the phone, as soon I understood why I felt so exhausted. Under me, there was a huge pool of blood, and I was sure that it was not from someone else. As I tapped the seat of the car with my right hand, the whole hand was soaked in blood, a sign that I had lost at least a litre of blood after the accident.

"Ohh shit!" I sighed and fell on my back.

At that point, my phone fell from my hands and I was at God's mercy. I remember nothing of what happened next, who saved me or how the whole thing happened. When I finally opened my eyes, thank God that happened; I was in the hospital, lying on a bed in a room with another man who looked like he had a broken hand or something.

I looked around for a while, as I tried to understand what was going on with me or where I was; a nurse popped up eventually and she told me that there was someone looking for me.

Clearly, I had undergone some type of surgery as my brain felt as if it had been beaten-up, due to the anaesthetic, and I could barely process a few words at a time.

"Who is it?"

The nurse smiled at me, she then looked into the hallway. "Sir, you can come in now!"

Alexandros stood at the door; I could not believe my eyes. I felt ashamed as well as relieved to see him there.

"God, how did you know I was here?" I muttered, as I struggled to turn my head towards him.

"I'd come for you to the end of the world if I had to ... you know that."

Those words came with a kiss on my forehead, and suddenly all my pain went away!

The Hospital

Confused and aching with every bone in my body, I looked at Alexandros as if he had been sent to me from the heavens. During those moments of rout and utter fear, his presence felt like the greatest relief a man could feel. Clearly, it is not easy to be alone, I understood that too well, right after I opened my eyes. The doctors and the nurses took good care of me, but my soul was craving for a familiar face, and Alexandros had come to see me at just the right time.

"How are you feeling?" he asked me in a soothing voice, right after he sat at the edge of the bed and grabbed my right hand to caress it.

"Alive, thank goodness …" I gasped. The pain was still there with me, reminding me every second how lucky I was to be alive. "The doctors told me I was lucky to still be breathing, judging how the car wreck looked; I guess I had a guardian angel hovering over my shoulder and that's why I can still talk to you now."

I tried to smile as I finished saying those things, but even that was too painful for me, and all I ended up doing was a twisted grimace.

"Hey, hey … calm down. You need to rest."

Alexandros said these things in my best interest, but I could not help but notice how he squeezed his other hand into a fist with anger.

At first, I thought he blamed himself for not being there to take care of me; especially after the fight we had. I did not expect him to do anything of the sort; for all the wrong reasons I had been a jerk to him. I knew now that I shouldn't have behaved or spoken to him in the way I did.

"God damn! ..." he ground his teeth and I felt bound to try and appease his anger.

"Alexandros, please don't blame yourself for what happened; there's nothing you could have done ... maybe God wanted this to happen, so that I would open my eyes to what is really important in my life ... and that is you!"

He looked at me with those dark brown watery eyes of his as the words coursed through his mind, but they did not come out. It felt as if he just could not make up his mind.

"If we didn't have that fight ... in the first place..." he sighed. "I should have ... you know, I'm sure that I would have gone with you to the airport."

I cut him short right there as I could not bear to see him blaming himself like that.

"Hey, and do what? End up together in the hospital? No thank you. I would rather know that you are safe and sound. I'll get back to my former self, I know I will and believe me we'll fix things!"

Alexandros' eyes were filled with disbelief at my words. For some reason, he looked at me as if he could see right through me. He clenched his teeth, and squeezed his eyes shut as if he were in pain.

"It's not safe, Mike ..." he started to say, but he stopped himself.

I was left up in the air as I had no idea what he was talking about.

"Safe where?" I mumbled and I looked straight into his eyes, begging for an answer.

"Here, in the hospital, on this forsaken island ... the whole of Greece, I don't know. You need to go home, and take care of yourself."

I gasped with a painful smile. "Go home? Are you crazy? I can barely move … I'm not going anywhere until I get better. I'm about to crawl my way back to the continent and make things worse for myself, in the process."

Alexandros was exasperated with my attitude; for some reason, he behaved as if I was supposed to understand something that he was not telling me.

"There has to be a way for you to get back. I don't know … an ambulance … a helicopter … something."

"You are making me laugh," I replied with a smile on my lips. "If only that were possible. You couldn't fathom the cost of such a stunt. I'm not a billionaire, you know, to rent a charter in order to get to a hospital five thousand miles away. We have to be realistic here."

Alexandros seeing that his argument was impossible, jumped as if burnt from the bed and he knelt on the floor with his face towards me.

"Why won't you listen to me? I have the best intentions at heart."

"And I believe you do, yet I cannot understand the secrecy behind them. Why should I leave when I've barely got here and the good doctors here are taking great care of me?"

"You don't understand, Mike!" he lashed back at me as if I had wronged him in some way. "This did not happen because you had bad luck … don't you get it?"

"Pardon me?" I reacted in my confusion because I really didn't understand what the hell was going on anymore. "What do you mean? Tell me the whole truth goddamn it!"

My sudden burst of anger caused me to forget my suffering as I unconsciously tried to get up onto my elbows. Yelling at him had caused my lungs to feel as if they were breaking into a thousand pieces. The pain that followed reminded me sharply of my precarious condition and I fell back onto the hospital bed aching in my misery and in my pain.

"Ahhh … God, my bones feel as if they have all been broken." I muttered, almost to myself, but Alexandros had picked up on it immediately.

"Hey, hey … calm down," he begged me as he came closer. "You are not allowed to make such sudden moves."

"You don't say?" I turned my head away from him. "I thought that you came here to comfort me, not to scare me."

He wept as he knelt at the side of my bed. His eyes told a different story though; as if a war went on inside his head. He tried to hide it from me to the best of his ability.

"I haven't, I am sorry …" he muttered, and he grabbed my feeble hand again. As he looked me straight in the eye, he said, "I care for you, more than you think; despite our fights and our disagreements. I can only see my future with you."

It sounded like a love statement to me. I enjoyed it and I hoped to hear some more, but at that point, a lovely nurse walked into my room with a syringe in her left hand and a box of pills in her right hand.

Her wide smile, rosy cheeks, and her white uniform were there as if to make me forget my pain. I fucking hated needles, but I had no other choice but to take it lying down; after all, it was for my own good, as I did not plan on lying on that bed for too long.

"Butt to the side please." She smiled as if she rejoiced in touching my round butt cheeks.

Judging from the way she took all the time in the world to give me that shot, I guess she enjoyed doing it. Too bad for her as she didn't know I was gay, and that nothing could happen between us, in this world or in the next.

As soon as that nasty part was done, she left, but not before winking at me. I tried to thank her in Greek, but I only knew a little, so Alexandros did it for me. I could barely think in my own language let alone speak a foreign language with the craziest alphabet.

"I think she has a crush on you already." Alexandros teased me, but I would not hear of it.

"Don't be foolish Alexandros. You know I am not into women, and I am sure she knows that already. Now, let's get back to what you were saying?" I added.

I could see how his face had suddenly changed; from light and smiling to dark and serious.

"You need to go!" he insisted again. It now started to annoy me.

"Again, with that shit?" I ground my teeth. "You're telling me to do something, but you are not telling me why. I won't hear another word from you about leaving. I am serious!"

"That was no accident!" Alexandros yelled with a fixed stare.

His face looked as if the heaviest weight had just been lifted off his shoulders. His eyes were still clouded and scared, but the breakthrough had occurred.

"What do you mean? I am feeling the effects right now; you didn't see the cab; it was a total wreck."

He kept on shaking his head. "You don't understand, Mike. I didn't say that the accident didn't occur. I am saying that someone planned for this to happen. You were a target and you are lucky to be alive as the aim was to kill you."

I lay there on that hospital bed, immobilized and I felt my heart begin to freeze. An eerie sense of unstoppable fear slowly overtook me, as I struggled to understand what someone might have against me. As far as I knew, I had not harmed anyone, at least not knowingly. I struggled to grasp the danger I found myself in.

"B … but, who … w … why? I don't understand?" I stuttered in a half-paralyzed voice. "I have never hurt anyone. Why would someone want to kill me? I am just a random tourist on the island like everyone else."

Alexandros sighed heavily. "You might think that way, but you could not be farther from the truth, Mike. You need to get off the island as soon as possible."

In an instant, my fear turned to anger. I could feel my blood as it boiled in my veins, and the reason was clearly Alexandros' secrecy. Clearly, he knew something but did not want to tell me the truth. I had no idea what he thought he was doing; maybe he thought he protected me, but instead, he hurt me more than the physical wounds on my body were.

This lack of trust felt like pouring salt into an open wound. I could not understand why he hid this from me anyway. The harm had been done, at least I had the right to know why I had almost died.

"For fuck's sake Alexandros!" I yelled at him. The sound of my angry voice carried through the closed door, echoing in the hallways. "If I am going to die anyway, at least tell me what I am dying for; that's the least you can do for me. I deserve to know the truth. I demand you tell it straight to my face, right goddamn now!"

Alexandros cried right there in front of me. "Mike, dearest, you know that I cannot do that … I do not have the heart for it."

"You don't?" I lashed out at him. "Then, get the fuck out my room! You are no use to me anyway … GO! I don't want to see your face right now!"

"Please don't push me away …" he begged but I didn't even look at him.

"I am not … you're doing it with your shitty actions. You said you loved me more than anything else in this world. Well, let me break it down to you, 'my love'; people who love each other never hide secrets from one another, regardless of the reasons and the 'presumed' best intentions."

That was the moment I turned my face away from him, and I expected him to say something in an attempt to defend himself against my accusations. He didn't as his phone started to ring at that moment.

I couldn't help but notice his horrified face the moment he picked up the phone. A sense of curiosity quickly engulfed me, and I wished I knew who called him, but my overblown sense of pride prevented me from uttering a single word. Maybe it was better that way, for both of us.

Alexandros didn't let the phone ring for too long as he cut the call. He put the phone back in his pocket.

"I have to go …" he said breathing hard. And then he left.

No goodbye, no kiss or other pleasantries … the sort we used to have whenever we met; either at the club or at the hotel. This time, he turned around and he gave me a cold look as he exited the room.

"Yeah … fuck off!" I muttered to myself, angrily as soon as he was gone.

My ego told me that I had done the right thing to push him away as he was disloyal, but at the same time, I couldn't help but feel a sense of regret.

Shallow tears ran down my face. I found myself in the most miserable place of my life, and I am not just referring to the hospital bed. Yeah, I hated the place too. The smell of chlorine, the white coats, and the needles; but at this time I was also an emotional wreck. I had no idea who I could trust anymore. I felt alone, abandoned in the claws of a wretched fate that rejoiced in tormenting me and ripping my soul to pieces.

Alexandros was the only person who I had close to me on Mykonos, except for Bruno and Daan. They were fine guys, but we had only spent a few moments together and I could hardly call them friends. The rest of my acquaintances were only temporary encounters, I could expect nothing from them. I was truly alone now that Alexandros had left … going to God knows where.

Despite the dark place I found myself in, I did not plan to call him. I have already told you that I have an ego the size of a mountain. I could have died right there on that hospital bed. I would still not pick up the phone from the nightstand. That's how stubborn I could get at times.

I spent the next few hours musing about my situation, but also about Alexandros' strange attitude towards me. I tried to figure-out the path that I should follow next, but my tired brain could not reach any logical conclusions. Tired, stressed-out and over my head, I decided that it was time for a few moments of rest. I needed sleep more than anything else. I tried to close my eyes and to stop thinking about anything at all.

My plans were simple enough, but little did I know that Karma had other plans in store for me. I guess only a few minutes after my attempting to sleep I heard my phone beep once. It was a text message. With great effort, I opened my eyes halfway to check and see who had the courage to disturb my slumber.

Something told me, it had to be Alexandros as there couldn't be anyone else but him calling, and I was right. As I turned on the screen his name popped up. I figured he had sent me an apology text or something. I imagined he felt sorry for having such a bitchy attitude towards me and that he wanted to fix things … or something like that.

I could not be farther from the truth; instead of an apology, I receive a scary text from him, almost on the brink of lunacy.

'Are you okay, Mike? Please text me back if you are still there. Please do it right now!"

'What the fuck?' I thought to myself as I re-read that text ten times. 'What now?'

I thought of texting him back to ask him what the hell was going on with him, but this fucked up, crazy attitude of his had started to bring out the worst in me. I was sick of this pointless game he played with me; I wanted it to end. Angry as I was, I threw the phone under the bed …

"Fuck you and your texts!" I ground my teeth and I turned onto the other side of my pillow.

Now, I was more than ever determined to sleep, despite being a ton of nerves; this was no easy stunt to pull off for me, regardless of the fact that I closed my eyes and struggled not to think of him. The struggle was in vain, without a doubt.

"What the hell is wrong with you man …" I wept in my solitude; my voice was ragged now and my heart ached. "Can't you see that I'm almost crippled now … what else do you want?"

Part of me wished that Alexandros could hear my sorrow, but he was not unfortunately there with me. The pain seemed to intensify in those moments as my nerves were stretched to their limit. I grabbed the white fluffy pillow and I covered my head with it, pulling it down over my head hard with my hands as hard as my aching muscles could bear.

"Fuck …!"

I suddenly heard the handle of the door; someone disturbed my sorrow. I swear at first, I thought that it was only my sick imagination. Reality soon crept on me as I could hear footsteps. My first instinct was that my lovely nurse had come to check on me. When Alexandros had come to visit me, she would always let me know first, and since this did not happen now, I figured that this was no 'external' visitation.

As I took my head from under the pillow, I could not believe my eyes; Bruno and Daan sat a few feet away from me, both were smiling and holding flowers. I did not think about the oddness of the situation neither I did think of how they had known in the first place that I was in the hospital. My loneliness had clouded my judgment, and I couldn't care less how or why they were there, as long as I was not alone anymore.

Their broad smiles were almost contagious, and their eyes seemed not to hide anything suspicious.

"God Mike, you look awful!" Bruno said, with a smile, as he came closer to the bed to offer me the stunning bouquet of golden daisies.

It was clearly supposed to be a funny remark meant to appease my aching heart. It did have the expected effect on me, but more than that, their pleasant attitudes had a soothing effect.

"Please, don't remind me. I know the shit I am in right now. It's not my best day for sure."

I tried to look cool and resilient, and there was a certain amount of sarcasm to my words, but I have no idea how I looked in their eyes. Daan approached the opposite side of the bed from where Bruno sat. His smile persisted as he sat on the edge of the bed; I tried to move a little to make some room for his huge stature, but I felt immense pain in the process.

"Please, don't trouble yourself too much, there is enough space for this old body to sit." He reacted, and I felt bad for being so incapacitated in front of their eyes.

"I just wanted to make sure you had enough room," I mumbled as my senses were distracted by the beautiful smells that emanated from the daisies Bruno had brought me.

"Please…" I said my eyes glued to the bouquet. "Can I hold them?"

Bruno quickly handed them to me so that I could smell their wonderful perfume. It felt incredibly refreshing as the odor drifted up through my nostrils I could feel the perfume as it touched and healed the wounds of my aching heart.

"Thank you so much. I did not think you would come to visit," I babbled, struggling not to blush too much.

"That's the right thing to do for a friend," Bruno replied, and he came to sit next to me. "So, how are you feeling? Is it that bad?"

I tried to smile. "It's not that bad; one little scratch is not going to break me." I bravely uttered but I knew that it was lies that came out of my mouth. The scars were only on the outside, carving nasty memories on the surface of my skin; what lay inside was more complicated and I could not even tell the full extent of the damage.

"That's good to hear actually," Daan replied. "We wish you a fast recovery … you're stronger than you look."

He nudged me as he said those words and I could feel that gentle push to the marrow of my aching bones. I tried to hide my instant grimace, but I had no idea how much success I had in my endeavor.

"Ahh, I hope you're right about that, ha-ha."

The atmosphere inside my hospital room had become relaxed. This was exactly what I needed to forget my episode with Alexandros. Smiling faces surrounded me and I swear the flowers had brightened my day in a way that thought would never happen. It looked as if my day had taken a turn for the better, or so I thought.

Moments later, as if a switch had been switched on, both Bruno and Daan's faces became preoccupied. I thought at first, that they wanted to leave as they had somewhere to go and they did not want to upset me by telling me, but it seemed I was wrong in my assumption.

"So, did you talk to your friend Alexandros after the accident?"

Bruno's question came out of the blue. It caught me by surprise and I didn't know what to say at first. Their sudden interest in Alexandros managed to awaken in me a series of questions and suspicions and then it hit me that they were involved with drugs. The thought scared me slightly as I did not understand what my role was in all of this. Why would they ask me if they could just call him and ask.

I had to lie. I didn't know the reason behind their question. I had to protect myself. Heck I could not run with my limp legs, so I was kind of stuck.

"No, I haven't … I don't know where he is. We have not spoken for a few days."

My eyes had become scanners, ready to record any suspicious reaction.

"I told you we shouldn't have come here!" Daan suddenly lashed out at Bruno who had turned his back on him.

"Shut the fuck up!" Bruno retorted.

"What if he's lying? Did you ever think about that?" Daan replied angrily.

I was now caught in a feud that I had nothing to do with, and as the situation grew more and more strange to me, I suspected the worst.

"Excuse me? Who is lying?" I asked them both, but I got no reply.

Bruno looked at Daan angrily, but no words came out of his mouth.

I insisted. "Hey, I am talking to you! What the hell is going on in here?"

It was ab ad move on my part!

"Shut the fuck up, Mike!" Daan yelled at me and he grabbed my right arm and squeezed it. The pain was fucking unbearable.

"Hey, let go of me! What the hell is wrong with you?"

Daan's anger was directed at me now. He had completely forgotten about Bruno. Both his hands were around my neck and he started to strangle me.

"You're going to spit it all out, you nasty piece of shit!" Daan yelled.

His face had turned devilish. It was something I had never seen in my life. I was surprised yet frightened at the same time, as never in my life had I been forced to face such a complicated situation. It did not look good for me, at all!

"Hey, Hey, Guys, what is going on in here? Why are you so angry suddenly?" I asked them in the kindest voice I could muster. There was no way for them to calm down, though, and I wished I knew what bothered them.

"Shut the fuck up, Mike with all your stupid questions and tell us where Alexandros is at the moment; or else ..." Bruno threatened me as he came closer to my bed.

I tried to pull back, as he came menacing towards me, but I had little room to maneuver. I was at their mercy and I was scared beyond words.

"OR ELSE WHAT?" I replied in a shock voice. "What the fuck are you going to do to me? I told you already I have no idea where he is. Why do you think I would lie to you anyway?"

Daan took a seat next to me on the bed. His face was rather serene with a wide smile that covered his face from ear to ear. I knew that was not his usual smile, I could tell from the previous encounter that there was something strange about this Dutch man. He had the facial expression of a man who wanted to stab you in the back the moment you tried close your eyes.

"Look, Mike ..." he started speaking in a seemingly kinder voice. "We have not come here to cause you any trouble, okay? We know that Alexandros was here to visit you earlier today."

I interrupted him briefly at this point. "I did not try to deny it. I told you he was here but then he left and he did not tell me where he was going. I did not even bother to ask him anyway. I don't care. He's a big man. He can handle his own business without me sticking my nose in."

Daan's grimace told of his frustration. He looked me in the eyes, and he sighed as if he tried to rearrange the thoughts in his head.

"All right! All right! I get it!" Daan smiled again, as he showed me his perfect white teeth. Bruno on the other hand, had started to lose his shit only two feet away and he could barely keep his words in.

"Ohh fuck this, Daan! Are we going to play around with this cunt until the end of days?" He had reacted angrily, but Daan threw him an angry look.

"Shh ... I've got this. Shut the fuck up and let me handle it."

I was now caught in something that I didn't even understand. I looked at them in turn; as I tried to gather something from their expressions, but I only got a sort of bipolar freak show that scared me even more. From anger to confusion, grimaces and smiles that had nothing to do with being happy. It was all there, and it was probably meant to scare the shit out of me.

Daan's turned attention back to me now, and I could tell he that he waited for an answer I did not have.

"So, are you going to tell me what I want to know or … should we try the hard way?" he said, with an evil look in his eyes.

I almost lost my fucking breath at that point. If I could run, I guess I'd have run a thousand miles away from that hospital; but unfortunately, I was pinned down, and at the mercy of these fucking freaks.

For a moment, I thought of pushing the panic button that was only inches away from my right hand, but they would surely see, and only God knew what they would do to me once I tried that 'sneak attack'.

"The hard way. What the fuck does that even mean? I told you I don't know anything!" I replied, with some strength in my voice.

Scared as I was, I did want to assert at least some small level of dominance. I did not want to appear weak in their eyes, but I had no idea how successful I actually was.

"Let's pray to God, that it won't come to that. It's better for you if you just tell us what we want to know, willingly. You would spare all of us a lot of trouble."

"I told you already, I don't know shit!" I ground my teeth at Daan and I wished that I could do more than that.

Bruno, on the other hand had already lost his patience. He started to pace back and forth in the room with his arms crossed.

"We are wasting our time here, Daan!" he yelled. "Can't you see that you will never be able to get anything out of him even if you talk nicely to him. I can smell his lies a mile away!"

Daan did not agree, but that was of little importance as Bruno had other plans … and they were rather nasty, at least where I was concerned. Daan tried to reply, but Bruno did not wait; instead he took action on his own. I did not expect him to do anything, at least not yet, and for that reason, he kind of caught me off-guard.

As I lay on the bed, with my head resting partly on the pillow, I found myself being pushed. Bruno grabbed my shoulders with both his hands, and he smashed me once against the mattress. The bed squeaked as if it was about to break. Even Daan jumped away at that moment, so I was left to fight the battle alone.

I was surprised by the speed of Bruno's movement; no more than a split second passed and I found my face covered with the pillow I had been resting my head on, just moments before. I struggled to fight back, and I grabbed his arms, but this was a disproportionate fight. He pressed down on my face with all the force he could muster and I could hear ...

"I'll fucking kill you ... motherfucker! You think you're smart, huh? I'll show you how it feels to be smart ... and dead, right now!"

My indistinct groaning, that replaced the screams I wanted to shout did not impress either of them at all. I could not feel Daan moving in any way, and he was not saying anything either. I was truly on my own now, as I fought for my life; the odds looked rather grim unfortunately, as I had only seconds left to live without the air that I desperately needed.

"That's what you get for acting smart with me ..." were Brunos's last words before he finished me off.

I had not given up though, and my arms flew through the air in a desperate attempt to grab something, anything ... to strike this crazy fucking Dutchman with!

I guess God was on my side in that moment, as I think I must have touched the alarm button; that's my suspicion as only seconds away from dying, the nurse broke through the door of my room. Maybe it was pure chance, or maybe she heard the noises ... I would never know.

"What's going on in here?" She yelled in a scared voice.

At that moment, I was free to breathe in the sweetest air my lungs had ever felt; the long arm of death had been only inches away, and now just like Lazarus in the Bible, I had come back to life. No miracle this time, or maybe a small one, for me at least, as I had gotten to the point, right then, under that choking pillow where I thought I'd never get another chance.

Bruno shifted his attention to the nurse now. "Nothing to concern you. Get out of here!"

The poor woman, in her reckless bravery refused, probably as she had no idea of who or what she dealt with.

"This is a hospital, sir! How dare you tell me to get away from one of my patients!" She replied boldly as she walked up to him.

Daan stood on the other side of my bed and he watched the scene without saying a word. I had barely recovered from my trauma and I couldn't even see properly. I tried to warn her of the danger but I had no voice … I didn't even get a chance to catch my breath.

"Fine!" Bruno smirked and that was all he said.

A second later, I saw as he smacked the poor nurse to the ground. She fell like a stone onto the floor.

"Aww fuck …" I said to myself, as I saw what had just happened. He would come back to me to finish the job. I could tell that this would happen and now there was no one to save me.

It was my luck that Daan freaked out then. "What the hell are you doing, man!" he yelled at Bruno and rushed to grab him as he was ready to smack the nurse again, right where she lay, almost dead on the floor.

"Take your hands off me!" Bruno replied, as he fought Daan. "I am sick of this shit already … I'll kill them all if I have to, and then I will get my hands on that bastard Alexandros!"

Daan pushed him out of the room with some effort. "Let's go. Goddamn it, before the cops get here. You want to sit in jail or what?"

"Take your fucking hands off me! I know what I am doing."

Bruno and Daan left the hospital without finishing the job they had started on me. I was lucky to be alive and I had no plans to let them get their hands on me for another second. I'd get my ass out of there as soon as I could get back on my feet.

I thought that someone would come in after Daan and Bruno were gone, but it did not happen as I expected. A few minutes passed and the nurse and I were alone inside that room. I still ached and she still lay unconscious on the floor. Her nose had been broken by Bruno's powerful blow, and now a trail of blood flowed onto the floor from the side of her right cheek.

"Poor soul …" I mumbled to myself.

I was aware that her sudden intervention had saved my life. I wished that I could do something for her in those moments, but I was too freaked out to know what to do. I was afraid for my own safety as well as no one could reassure me that those lunatics were not coming back soon.

With that thought in mind, I started to push against the bed with the little strength I had left. I was eventually successful as I had managed to stand up. My every step now felt like an ordeal, and the pain I felt was worse than anything I had ever felt before. I had no other chance though. I had to go now or remain there and face my end.

A last gaze at the nurse's body almost caused me to shed a tear. I felt for her, I was not a selfish man, but I could not help her, much as I wanted to. My clothes were somewhere in the hospital, but I did not have time for such luxuries. All I managed to take with me was my phone and the gown that the hospital had given me when they were done with me in the operating room.

The walls of those interminable corridors were of great help to me, as they offered me support whenever I was about to fall. I pushed myself again and again until I finally managed to reach the elevator. I peeked back for a moment to see if there was anyone coming, but the whole place looked deserted. The atmosphere seemed to be just before a great hurricane hit.

I gasped with pain as I pushed the button. No thoughts ran through my head of where to go next or what to do. All I knew then was that I wanted to get as far away as possible from that place. The destination didn't matter much, as long as I could get to somewhere safe.

I walked out of the hospital, limping as I struggled to stand. I needed great effort to perform the task, but I would not give up, no matter what. As I reached the main street, I immediately started to look for a taxi. My shortness of breath had caused me a lot of trouble. I felt exhausted and I could barely see for any distance.

Luckily, a car had approached, and, in my desperation, I almost jumped in front of the car, right there in the middle of the road.

People looked at me now from all directions as if I were some lunatic who had escaped from the madhouse. I couldn't care less; I was desperate to get out of there.

The moment the driver pushed the brake pedal, I could hear the tires as they screeched on the hot asphalt. A man put his head out of the window and he started to curse me; probably in Greek. I did not understand a damn thing, but that didn't worry me.

I gasped, in a broken voice. "Hey! … ! Please, I need a ride … I need it!"

Luckily, the driver was a reasonable man and he got out of the car to help me. He probably saw how fucked up I was for sure. He could see that I didn't need any trouble from him.

"Are you okay?" he asked, and I just nodded without saying a word.

"I need to get out of here … I'll pay as much as you want!"

My reply did not connect with reality as I didn't have a fucking dime on me. All my belongings except for my phone was still in the hospital and that included all my cash and my cards. I was penniless now, and I was not even aware of it.

"Come, let me help you get into the car," he offered and I accepted without hesitation as I was in no position to argue.

I grabbed his right arm and I crawled onto the back seat of his car.

The moment my ass landed on that leather surface I felt the greatest relief of my life. I had never thought that sitting down could provide so much comfort for my aching body. My bones and my muscles were traumatized and even breathing felt like an ordeal. I took a moment to recover from all the effort of getting out of the hospital room and onto the road.

"Where to?" the driver asked me before our ride started.

I did not hear him at first, as my mind struggled on so many levels. I thought of a thousand things at the same time. Alexandros was surely the main dish on the menu, but I also struggled to find a way to get back home without having to face Bruno and Daan again. Those crazy bastards seemed quite dangerous to me now, especially after they had tried to kill me and only by the grace of God I had gotten away from them.

"Sir? Where do you want to go?" the man insisted, seeing my lack of response.

This second question woke me up from my trance. I shook my head twice as I tried to make sense of reality, but even that simple gesture felt too painful.

"Ugh … let me think," I mumbled. I had no idea where to go, then a thought struck me. I would call Alexandros!

I grabbed my phone from the back seat. It had little battery left but it was still enough for a few calls.

"Please wait a minute, sir!" I said.

My hand shook as I pushed the button to call Alexandros; the phone rang a few times, but it looked as if my friend had no intention to answer for some reason.

"Aw fuck … Alexandros! What the hell are you doing?" I muttered to myself with frustration.

"To my hotel, please …" I said and then I gave him the address.

I had checked out already, but I was sure that I could find some understanding; if I had to. I would tell them that I had forgotten something inside the room that I needed to recover urgently.

The car started to drive as I tried to get some order into my thoughts. It looked damn complicated to solve anything without any money and with two crazy fuckers still on my tail.

Every now and then, the driver would look at me in his rearview mirror. I am sure that he smelt something fishy about this whole deal. I was dressed in a hospital gown, looking like shit and with no idea where to go. I was afraid that he would call the cops because of what he had witnessed. This would surely cause Alexandros even more of a problem as they would force me to testify.

The last thing I wanted for my friend was for him to end up in prison. Despite being a jerk to me at times, I still cared for him.

A few minutes into our ride the phone started to ring. I quickly grabbed it and I saw that it was Alexandros.

"Thank God!" I exclaimed with such intensity that I even grabbed the driver's attention for a moment.

"Hey man, where the hell are you? Why didn't you pick up when I called you?"

I had caught Alexandros off guard the second I answered the call. He did not get a chance to say a thing.

"I did not have my phone on me. What is it?" he asked, and I could tell from his voice that he was startled.

"Those fuckers tried to kill me!" I almost shouted through the phone. "I am lucky to be alive!"

"What!"

"You heard me, they tried to fucking kill me ... because of you."

Alexandros sounded petrified on the phone. "Who tried to kill you?"

"Bruno and Daan ... who the fuck else. They tried to strangle me and then they tried to smother me with the fucking pillow, inside the hospital, Goddamn!"

"My God ... I didn't think they would go that far." He replied in shock.

"Yeah, looks like they like to travel a lot ... no kidding."

"Where are you right now? Are you okay?" Alexandros asked with a scared voice.

I sighed. "I am in a cab. I don't even know where the fuck I am going; and yeah, I am still breathing so this is a good thing. Where the hell are you?"

"Ugh, I can't tell you ..." he mumbled, almost embarrassed and that really caused me to lose my shit.

"You what? You fucking bastard, I almost got killed because of you and you can't tell me where you are. What kind of sick shit is this?"

I yelled at him at the top of my lungs; I could not believe that Alexandros acted so secretively towards me after all I had been through because of him.

"Mike, please calm down!" He added, but it was impossible for me to do so.

"I won't calm down, goddamn it! I can't!" I yelled back at him. "I am lucky to be alive and now you're telling me to calm down? How the fuck am I supposed to do that?"

"I don't want to get you into any more trouble; trust me, I know what I am saying!" he replied, but I found it hard to believe him.

"More trouble than I already had. You have got to be kidding me. You'd better show your face in the next ten minutes, or I'm going to slit your fucking throat with my bare hands when I see you."

I was in no condition to even slap someone, but I was too angry to not say something to him after all I had suffered because of him.

"Fine, fine ... we will meet at the beach ... our beach, if you remember, you'll find me by that small tavern."

"Fuck your secrecy," I replied angrily, "and that small Tavern!"

"You know where to go." Alexandros said to me, shortly, before he ended the conversation.

"Can you believe this shit? He hung up on me!" I mumbled in a schizophrenic voice, and the cab driver thought that I had spoken to him, but in fact, I hadn't. He looked at me for a moment though, and I guess he wanted to say something, but he eventually refrained from opening his mouth altogether. It was better that way for all of us!

I gave him the address of the beach that Alexandros had spoken about. Going to my hotel was out now, as I needed some answers and I needed them soon. I did not know how long I was going to last in the fucking darkness that Alexandros had pushed me into.

Now, I was even more eager to find my answers. I was eager to draw my next breath but my rib cage hurt like hell, so breathing was not fun for me right now. It was more like a sacrifice I had to do to stay alive.

As soon as we reached the beach, I realized that I had no money on me. I felt embarrassed as shit, especially as the cab driver looked at me as if I were some sort of broke-ass trickster.

"It will be 17 Euros!"

Those words rang like a bell in my head. My eyes scanned the area as I hoped to find Alexandros there so that he could give me money to pay the man.

"A moment, please sir; my friend should be able to give me some cash and then I'll pay you." I replied embarrassed.

"Fine, but I can't wait here the whole day," he replied, almost grinding his teeth.

"You won't, I promise!"

Luckily, Alexandros, had appeared out of nowhere. I then, opened the door of the taxi and I yelled at him.

"Come on man; I need some money to pay for the cab."

Alexandros kept looking back as he approached the car, as if he tried to make sure that no one followed him.

"How much do you need?" he asked as he dug through his pockets.

"Just give him twenty … and help me get out of this car."

As soon as the cab driver was paid, he drove away furiously. Alexandros on the other hand, looked at me with a puzzled look in his eyes.

"Man, you look like shit. Why did you leave the hospital?"

"Are you fucking deaf? I told you that Bruno and Daan tried to fucking kill me. They even knocked out a nurse on their way out. If it were not for that poor soul entering the room when she did, they would have finished choking me to death."

"Fuck!" he muttered looking down.

"And all because of you!" I added, to torment him and to make him feel guilty.

"What did they want from you, anyway?"

I sighed as I struggled to find my balance. I leaned on his shoulder.

"They asked me about you … where you were and all that shit. When I told them, I didn't know anything, they tried to kill me, if you can imagine that."

Alexandros looked at me horrified as the tears almost poured down his frozen cheeks.

"They did what?"

I scoffed. I tried not to look at him as I did not like to see Alexandros that way, despite it all being his fault.

"Yeah, they tried to strangle me to death. Bruno to be more precise as Daan had a more 'friendly' approach to the whole situation, if I may say so."

"My God, I did not think that the bastards would come to that … I am going to fucking kill them. I don't give a fuck! No one has the right to lay a finger on you."

Alexandros' horror soon turned to unstoppable anger. He turned his face towards me then, as he tried to conceal his tears in the process. His beautiful brown eyes burnt with fury now.

"Where are they now? I am going straight … I'll teach these bitches a lesson!"

"Hey, hey, calm down!"

I grabbed Alexandros' right arm and I could feel as he shook with anger.

"What do you think you are doing?"

"They tried to kill you; goddamn it! Does this seem a little thing to you!" He shouted at me as he tried to pull away from me. Clearly, my friend was at his wits end, and he now acted crazy.

I could not hold my grip for too long and soon he was free. He grabbed his head with both his hands, and he kept cursing as he paced back and forth.

"I'll fucking kill them … I don't give a fuck what is going to happen next. These bastards deserve to die for what they did!"

My body ached like hell, and I struggled to come up with a way to help Alexandros calm down. I walked up to him and I tried to look into his eyes. This was no easy task to perform in my condition.

"Alexandros …" I said, but he didn't even look at me. At that moment he was caught up in his own vengeful world.

"ALEXANDROS!" I yelled at him a second time, as I hoped that my loud voice would catch his attention.

This time, he looked at me for a moment but he did not say a word. I took advantage of this opportunity, I decided to grab my chance.

"Look at me!" I yelled. Luckily there was no one around to hear me shouting. "I am still in one piece; I am fucking breathing. I'll be fine in a week or two! Why sacrifice the rest of your life for something that can be avoided. We are not the mob here to set an example; just let them be, we'll go away so they'll never be able to track us ever again."

Alexandros listened to my words in silence, but I couldn't tell if any of them pierced the thick membrane of ignorance that surrounded his heart at that moment. I felt his urge to punish those Dutch bastards, I really did, but it was not worth it in the end as that would only complicate our lives ... and for no good reason, at that.

"Do you understand my point?" I insisted after a few seconds to make sure he that had actually listened to me.

Soon, I discovered that my hopes to sooth his pain were in vain. Alexandros scoffed and his face was still wrinkled with pain and anger.

"You're fine you say, Mike?" I shrugged not knowing what to say. "Look at you, goddamn it! You can barely stand, and your neck looks like hell. You're lucky to be alive right now and all because of me. You did nothing wrong to those bastards and still they targeted you, thinking that they could reach me that way."

Right then a police car with its sirens blaring passed by and for a moment my heart almost froze with fear.

"Alexandros ... you can't stay in the open like this; it's not safe." I replied in a ragged voice, but again he would not listen.

"I don't care; they can get me; I will tell them everything I know and everything I did. I am not afraid anymore, Mike. Not after what happened to you. Fuck the money and everything else. There's nothing in this world I would trade you for! Do you understand?"

Right when he dropped that last question, he grabbed my shoulder as if he were trying to shake me out of my 'safety' slumber. His grip was rather painful as my bones were still in the worst shape, they had ever been in.

I grimaced, almost instantly, and against my will, as I didn't want to show Alexandros that I suffered so badly.

"Ahh ..." The grinding of my teeth reached him. "I know, I know ... it's just ... I ..." I had run out of words; this was true and I just looked back at Alexandros.

"Oh God, I am so sorry, I did not mean to hurt you even more." He added the second he noticed my twisted expression.

"It's fine." I smiled back. Something deep inside me urged me to make him feel as comfortable as possible. "I told you, these physical wounds will heal soon enough. It's important that nothing else happens from now on."

Finally, Alexandros nodded in agreement. God knows, a huge weight was lifted off my chest when I saw his reaction.

"I am happy that you understand the true importance of things," I added happily and then I lost myself inside the warm embrace of his arms.

We stood there like that for a few good moments; no words were uttered as silence proved to be the best counselor. As strange as it might seem, in those moments of grief and pain I felt more connected to Alexandros than ever before. All the boundaries were broken down, now and we were truly breathing heart to heart, together.

"We need to take you home and change this nasty looking hospital gown to some proper looking clothes."

His suggestion sounded like the most brilliant idea and there was no way for me to refuse. Besides, my initial plan to go to the hotel was not that safe, since I did not have a room anymore; and God knew what reaction those people would have once they saw me dressed in that hospital gown. Calling the cops without me knowing did not sound so farfetched anyway now.

"You're right ... let's go," I replied with a smile. "I am feeling tired anyway. I think I need to lie down for a moment."

"Come, I have the car parked right around the corner." He added with a serious face.

"Hey, hey, hold on with the racing, you know I can't run that fast," I chuckled, trying to lighten the mood.

"Ohh, sorry, I forgot" he mumbled, and he unlocked the car.

With some effort, I managed to get in the front seat all by myself; my ribs still killed me every time I drew a breath, let alone when I made more sudden twisted moves. That was a curse I had to live with for a while, since doctors could not do much about it; ribs are the worst when it comes to breaking something in your body.

Alexandros started to drive; the road to his home was right along the shore of the Mediterranean; the scenery was absolutely breathtaking. Words were futile right now, so I kept my head stuck to the car window with my eyes lost in the distance towards the horizon that was reflected in that crystal-clear azure water. The waves were slowly bumping against the shore, with the calmness of a man who has lived through all the possible things in life and now understood the true meaning of life.

I tried not to think of the horror I had just been through, but my mind would not let me rest; that cursed subconscious pushed those recent nasty near-death memories out from under the rug of my mind. This constant battle went on inside my head and pushed the words out of my mouth ... the uncertainty I guess scared me the most. I had to ask.

"What now?"

My sudden words disturbed Alexandros' concrete like concentration. He removed his tense brown eyes from the road and looked at me for a moment.

"What do you mean?"

"I don't know," I mumbled. "You and I ... and ..."

A long pause followed as I struggled to put some order into my thoughts as they chased through my head each seemed to be equally important. I just could not decide on the order now.

"We're going to your house now; I get that ... but then? What's to happen to us?" I added, moments later, to which Alexandros could not find an answer to satisfy me yet.

He shrugged, in return, and then he gave me a long gaze that seemed to show the emptiness inside him. His left hand held the steering wheel tightly while his left reached across to touch mine.

"I can't tell you anything right now," he muttered in a sooth-ing voice this time. "All I know is that you and I will be okay! That's the one thing I do know!"

It was pretty confusing, if you ask me, but I could not help but smile back. His eyes were clearly clouded with things that didn't allow his soul to get the much needed peace he needed. I thought to ask him about it, but on reflection, I refrained from doing so.

The truth is, I was afraid of his reaction and of the lies he would tell me just so that I could calm myself. A different ap-proach was needed to appease his anger, but I had not reached that point just yet.

"I hope with all my heart that you are right about this one," I said, as my words sought his, confirmation. The eyes are in-deed the mirror to one's soul and few people can really conceal their true intentions as their eyes give them away. Alexandros was not one of those people, and I guess that was why he failed to make contact, on purpose.

"Don't worry," he replied after a deep breath. "I know what I am talking about."

With that, our conversation ended. I did not ask any more questions as I did not want to bother Alexandros any further. I chose to retreat to the 'comfort' of my own mind and try and resolve my own dilemmas. One thing was clear to me; I was caught up in a war that was not mine and one that I could not utterly understand.

Things went on around me that were rather overwhelming, and I struggled to keep my integrity together. With all the doubts and the questions clouding my brain, one thing was clear enough to me: Fuck Mykonos! I was going to leave that forsaken island without looking back. All I could pray for now was that noth-ing else 'unforeseen' happened to me on my way out. I would not be able to face yet another 'car accident'. I had barely walked out alive from the first one.

As soon as we reached Alexandros' home, I could feel that he was still restless. My eyes fell onto the sofa the moment we walked through the door of the apartment. Even bending my knees to sit down felt like torture, but I had no other choice. The surface of that couch felt way better than the car seat.

"God, this feels like a blessing!" I gasped and I stretched my head towards the red plush pillow.

"Do you need anything?" Alexandros asked as he walked back and forth through the room.

"Yeah, a new body if you could give me one that doesn't hurt so much; But make sure it's the same one as I don't want to lose this sexy ass for anything in the world."

This joke I had made in between sobs, touched my friend to some extent as I could see him smiling. That was a good thing, if you ask me, as I had not seen a genuine smile on his face for quite a while.

"You're right about that! It's sexy as hell, even when it's in pain."

"Some water if you have, as I feel as if I am choking on my own air," I replied.

Alexandros rushed to the fridge to bring me a bottle.

"Here you go! I hope it's not too cold, I just grabbed it from the fridge."

Cold as ice but I did not complain; the hot weather on that Greek island can make you sometime feel as if your skin is about to catch fire … and your lungs too. It is beautiful and deadly at the same time if you don't hydrate yourself properly. A few mouthfuls later and I could already feel how every cell of mine was being rejuvenated. Alcohol is good, but there are moments when pure water feels like manner straight out of heaven; right there on Alexandros' couch was that moment for me.

After handing me the small bottle of water, Alexandros disappeared into the kitchen. At first, I imagined that he needed a drink or something to eat, so I chose not to bother him in any way.

Minutes passed, and he failed to come back into the living room. I kept wondering what he did in there as he was not talking to me either. The dreaded silence made me sick, especially in those moments after all I had been through. Being alone was probably the worst fear I had acquired recently.

I dared to call his name eventually, despite all the risks. "Alexandros? Are you still there?"

He did not reply at first, and when I was about to call for him again, I could see him as he walked out of the kitchen. At the same moment, his phone went into his pocket and I could tell that he struggled to control his temper. His face was reddish despite his olive skin tone, I could still see the blood as it rushed under his skin.

"Is everything okay?" I asked him in a worried voice as I did not like the way he looked.

He obviously tried to lie to me. "Yeah, yeah, I just had some water and a sandwich. Do you want one too?"

I shook my head as hunger was not the thing that bothered me.

"Nah, I can barely feel my stomach right now, let alone hunger. I will let you know if anything changes, but for the moment I am good."

"Okay, just let me know. I'll bring you anything you need."

He smiled at me, but I could read the treachery behind it. He hid something from me and that kind of pissed me off.

"I will, don't worry …" I replied.

I tried to ask him something else, but he cut me off before I could open my mouth.

"Mike, ugh … I kind of have to go now, for an hour or so."

This took me by surprise; caught off guard as I was, I still found the strength to interrogate him …

"Alexandros, I hope you're not planning on doing something stupid."

He gave me an unusually straight face. Alexandros would usually have a cheeky grin on his face, but now he looked at me as if some cursed Titan had stolen his smile for eternity.

"I swear, to God!" he replied. "They are calling me to come into work. I will be back before you know it."

"But weren't the cops looking for you at Mykonian City pub? Why would you return there, so that you can get caught?" I insisted.

I had hoped that I could change his mind, but my efforts were of no use.

"They came once. It's not as if they are spending every day and night there." Alexandros smiled back to me, but I could find no comfort in it. "I will be safe. I know what I am doing."

I had never been so doubtful in my life! Alexandros had told me that he knew what he was doing, but what scared me the most was the fact that I had no idea what his true intentions were. I could bet the rest of my days on earth that he had lied to me. I did not unfortunately have a way to make him tell me the truth.

"I am begging you just be safe. I would never forgive myself knowing that I allowed you to harm yourself."

Seeing my concern, Alexandros walked up to me, and he leaned over to give me a sweet long kiss on the lips.

"Please, don't make this the last one!" I murmured. I hardly dared to look into his eyes.

"Don't worry so much about me; just have some rest until I get back."

"Yeah sure. I'll have a drink if you have some here," I replied with a gasp.

"Of course, I think I have a bottle of whiskey around somewhere. Let me bring it to you."

Alexandros went to look for it in the kitchen. To me it felt like an eternity until he came back with it.

"I feared I had finished it already, but here it is barely touched!" He smiled as he placed it on the small coffee table, along with a square glass. "Help yourself, but don't get wasted, okay?"

I grinned without saying a word. I was too busy pouring myself some of that fine-looking whiskey.

"I'll be back!" These were the last words my ears picked up from Alexandros' lips before he vanished through the door.

I was left alone with that promise on the couch. It looked like there was little for me to do from now on, therefore I returned to what I could do. I turned the TV on to a music channel, Greek of course, so there was little for me to understand. I went along with the vibe anyway, I had little interest in understanding the words if I was able to feel the rhythm.

A few whiskey glasses later I passed out on the couch. I was not extremely drunk, but the fatigue and the physical traumas had taken their toll on me. I didn't even know what time it was anymore. I just lost contact with reality and I drifted in a realm that was way too familiar to me. At this time, the inner mazes of my mind looked different from before. Dark Clouds sifted nightmares into my soul despite my struggle to fight back this nasty vibe.

From time to time, I would open my eyes and mumble some things that were undecipherable, even for me. I had not been a sleepwalker before, at least not from what I could remember, but these days nothing was normal anymore. My life and the whole fucking world that surrounded me had begun to transform into something hideous that scared the soul out of me.

My troubled slumber met its end eventually. A loud bang at the door of the apartment pushed all my senses to their breaking point. I opened my eyes automatically. I struggled to understand whether this was reality or just another nightmare. Instinctively, I touched the base of my neck with both my hands to make sure that I still breathed. I was unable to see if the marks left by Bruno were still there, but they were still painful to the touch.

This was reality without a doubt; a dream could never cause such pain. I didn't have time to figure it out because as soon as I turned my foggy eyes towards the door, I saw Alexandros fall to the floor. His yellow shirt was stained with blood to a frightening extent.

"Alexandros!" I screamed in horror and I jumped off the couch.

My body had miraculously forgotten the pain and it allowed me to react like a professional athlete at the Olympics. I rushed forward and I fell on my knees next to him.

"Alexandros, my God, what the hell happened?" I cried desperately and I tried to lift him up from the floor, but this sturdy Greek stallion weighed a ton.

I struggled to pull him towards me so that I could close the front door. Curious guests were the last thing we needed right now. During all this time, Alexandros kept smiling, almost to himself and there was an instance when his smile turned to crazed laughter.

"Alexandros what is going on? What have you done?"

My questions went unanswered but then as I pulled him a few feet towards me, I saw a gun emerge from beneath him. I was no gun expert, but this looked like a 45-caliber pistol, a lethal weapon that could kill a man with just one shot. I lost my breath as my eyes landed on the weapon.

"OH MY GOD!" I exclaimed and it looked as if Alexandros was coming back to his senses.

"Are you hurt?" I yelled at him, as I struggled with the last drops of energy I had left, to pull that shit away from him.

"I shot the motherfucker!" Alexandros rejoiced and this was followed by satisfied laughter. "I told him he couldn't fuck with us ... but he wouldn't listen. I'm sure I have convinced him now!"

At first, I thought he was delusional, but that wound on his arm was proof enough that something had happened.

"Alexandros! What have you done? We need to get you cleaned up ... call the ambulance or something!" I started to freak out as I saw the open wound on his left arm, near his shoulder.

"Help me up!" he said, looking straight into my eyes.

"I can barely stand myself." I muttered, but I struggled to pull him to his feet.

Alexandros stretched-out his right hand that had not been touched by a bullet; the blood was indeed coming from his wound, but it had stained his shirt so extensively that I thought that the wound would be the end of him. The bottle of whiskey was still half full on the coffee table, so he grabbed it and he started to pour it straight down his throat.

"I am sure this will help to kill the germs!" he muttered, and then he slammed the bottle down almost breaking it.

"What's with the gun? What have you done?" I insisted, as I was thirsty for the truth. "Since when do you wear a gun?"

"In this business, you cannot survive for a day if you don't have a gun!" he replied.

I was shocked at the ease when Alexandros spoke about guns. I looked at him as if the answer he had given me was not enough, but only the beginning of something more extensive.

"What business Goddamn it?"

"The drug business baby; that shit's worth millions. You need a way to protect it because otherwise suckers are going to steal it from you. But that's all in the past now. I will throw away the gun when this is done, I swear ..."

"You've thrown empty oaths at me quite often these days. What did you do?" I insisted and he continued to scoff at me.

"I told you I shot the bastard. He could not get away with trying to kill you so easily. He had to pay for it!"

"Bruno?" my jaw dropped.

Alexandros smirked. "That's right; that motherfucker is not going to bother us anymore; he's done."

"Did you kill him?" I screamed, "My God, have you lost your mind!"

"Don't freak out on me now. I shot him ... I saw him falling and yeah I did want to kill his ass and that's the honest truth."

EIN HERZ FÜR AUTOREN A HEART FOR AUTHORS À L'ÉCOUTE DES AUTEURS MIA KAPΔIA ΓIA ΣYΓΓ
...ΤΑ FÖR FÖRFATTARE UN CORAZÓN POR LOS AUTORES YAZARLARIMIZA GÖNÜL VERELIM SZ
...PER AUTORI ET HJERTE FOR FORFATTERE EEN HART VOOR SCHRIJVERS TEMOS OS AUT
...ZÖINKÉRT SERCE DLA AUTORÓW EIN HERZ FÜR AUTOREN A HEART FOR AUTHORS À L'ÉCOU
...ÇÃO ВСЕЙ ДУШОЙ К АВТОРАМ ETT HJÄRTA FÖR FÖRFATTARE À LA ESCUCHA DE LOS AUTO
...URS MIA KAPΔIA ΓIA ΣYΓΓPAΦEIΣ UN CUORE PER AUTORI ET HJERTE FOR FORFATTERE EEN
...ARIMIZA GÖN...ERE...ZÖINKÉRT SERCE DLA AUTORÓW EIN HERZ FÜ
...OR SCHRIJVERTTE...S O...ÇÃO ВСЕЙ ДУШОЙ К АВТОРАМ ETT HJÄRTA FÖ

The author

Michael Kopytko was born in October 1988. He
lives in Basel, Switzerland.
He was educated up to high school level. Michael
has his own company and works as a ghostwriter
helping people to apply correctly for jobs. Michael
writes CV's and motivational letters and prepares
applicants for their interviews.
His interests are travel and writing. 'Bar Tender' is
his first book.

The publisher

He who stops getting better stops being good.

This is the motto of novum publishing, and our focus is on finding new manuscripts, publishing them and offering long-term support to the authors.
Our publishing house was founded in 1997, and since then it has become THE expert for new authors and has won numerous awards.

Our editorial team will peruse each manuscript within a few weeks free of charge and without obligation.

You will find more information about
novum publishing and our books on the internet:

www.novum-publishing.co.uk